THROUGH THE MAGIC DOOR

Also by Sir Arthur Conan Doyle in
A COMMON READER EDITION:

The White Company / Sir Nigel

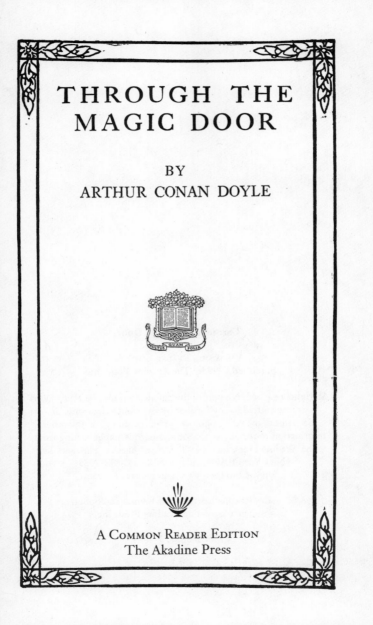

THROUGH THE
MAGIC DOOR

BY
ARTHUR CONAN DOYLE

A COMMON READER EDITION
The Akadine Press

Through the Magic Door

A COMMON READER EDITION
published 1999 by The Akadine Press, Inc.

A COMMON READER EDITION and fountain colophon are
trademarks of The Akadine Press, Inc.

ISBN 1-888173-98-X

2 4 6 8 10 9 7 5 3

INTRODUCTION

When I wrote the series of papers which have been published under the inclusive name of "Through the Magic Door" my idea was rather to address the young man of from 17 to 22 who was asking for some guidance in literary matters. In these days of cheap editions there is no one who cannot afford to have a small library of his own, and as a man's mind and character depend upon what he reads, it is very important that the bookshelf—even if it be in the singular—shall contain books that count. In dealing with the subject I have kept human limitations in mind, for indeed there is no surer way to disgust a youth with literature than to insist upon his taking nourishment which is beyond his digestion. Most of what I recommend is easily assimilated, and my comments and explanations may perhaps peptonize it still further.

I have found, as a matter of fact, that my recommendations and remarks have been taken seriously in far more exalted circles than any which I had originally in mind, and that scholars and thinkers have been good enough to say that I have thrown a new light upon their studies. Perhaps it is that I have been an omnivorous reader and very catholic in my tastes, so that I take a broad view even if it is not a very profound one. At any rate, the fact remains and I am proud to think that my rambling notes have had such an effect.

I suppose that twenty years have elapsed since the book came out, and yet, as I read it over, I do not find that there is much that I wish to change, though naturally there is much that I could add. It would be an admission that the years had been wasted were it not so. My life has taken a slant which has led me to explore deeply the literature of the occult, and this is so enormous, and, I may add, so enthralling, that it has limited my general reading. I love, however, always to have one big

book in the background in which I can take
refuge when my thoughts have tended to work
too much in narrow grooves of science or religion. Such a book at the present moment is
Guizot's History of France, the most readable
national history that I have met. There is a
Boston edition with glorious pictures which is
a perpetual joy. I have sat at an open win-
dow of the Biltmore Hotel, and with the constant roar of the trolley cars in my ears and
all the buzz of the great city around me, I
have forgotten all and found myself in the
forests of Gaul, or wandering the Old World
from Brittany to Asia Minor as did those wonderful old Barbarians, leaving afar off such
place names as Galicia to mark their passage.
How many know that when Saint Paul wrote
an epistle to the Galatians he was really writing to natives of what we now call France who
had fought and plundered until they had
reached this far-off settling place. The old
German hive too, with its constant swarming,
reacted centuries before Christ upon the na-

tions to the West of the Rhine, exactly as it did within the last few years. Cæsar drove them over the river even as Foch, Haig, and Pershing have done, and it is just the certainty that the old cycle will come round once more which causes all the fear and unrest of Europe to-day. These, however, are too grave thoughts for a preface, and so, with thanks for your company, I stand aside and turning the handle I swing the magic door back upon its hinges.

ARTHUR CONAN DOYLE.

THROUGH THE MAGIC DOOR

THROUGH THE MAGIC DOOR

I

I CARE not how humble your bookshelf may be, nor how lowly the room which it adorns. Close the door of that room behind you, shut off with it all the cares of the outer world, plunge back into the soothing company of the great dead, and then you are through the magic portal into that fair land whither worry and vexation can follow you no more. You have left all that is vulgar and all that is sordid behind you. There stand your noble, silent comrades, waiting in their ranks. Pass your eye down their files. Choose your man. And then you have but to hold up your hand to him and away you go together into dreamland. Surely there would be something eerie about a line of books were it not that familiarity has deadened our sense of it. Each is a mummified soul embalmed in cere-cloth and natron of leather and printer's ink. Each cover of a true book enfolds the concentrated essence of a man. The personalities of the writers have faded into the thinnest shadows, as their bodies into impalpable dust, yet here are their very spirits at your command.

It is our familiarity also which has lessened our perception of the miraculous good fortune which we enjoy. Let us suppose that we were suddenly to learn that Shakespeare had returned to earth, and that he would favor any of us with an hour of his wit and his fancy. How eagerly we would seek him out! And yet we have him—the very best of him—at our elbows from week to week, and hardly trouble ourselves to put out our hands to beckon him down. No matter what mood a man may be in, when once he has passed through the magic door he can summon the world's greatest to sympathize with him in it.

If he be thoughtful, here are the kings of thought. If he be dreamy, here are the masters of fancy. Or is it amusement that he lacks? He can signal to any one of the world's great story-tellers, and out comes the dead man and holds him enthralled by the hour. The dead are such good company that one may come to think too little of the living. It is a real and a pressing danger with many of us, that we should never find our own thoughts and our own souls, but be ever obsessed by the dead. Yet second-hand romance and second-hand emotion are surely better than the dull soul-killing monotony which life brings to most of the human race. But best of all when the dead man's wisdom and the dead man's example give us guidance and strength in the living of our own strenuous days.

Come through the magic door with me, and sit here on the green settee, where you can see the old oak case with its untidy lines of volumes. Smoking is not forbidden.

Would you care to hear me talk of them?
Well, I ask nothing better, for there is no volume there which is not a dear, personal friend,
and what can a man talk of more pleasantly
than that? The other books are over yonder, but these are my own favorites—the ones
I care to re-read and to have near my elbow.
There is not a tattered cover which does not
bring its mellow memories to me.

Some of them represent those little sacri-
fices which make a possession dearer. You
see the line of old, brown volumes at the bottom? Every one of those represents a lunch.
They were bought in my student days, when
times were not too affluent. Threepence was
my modest allowance for my midday sandwich
and glass of beer; but, as luck would have it,
my way to the classes led past the most fascinating bookshop in the world. Outside the
door of it stood a large tub filled with an ever-
changing litter of tattered books, with a card
above which announced that any volume
therein could be purchased for the identical

sum which I carried in my pocket. As I approached it a combat ever raged betwixt the hunger of a youthful body and that of an inquiring and omnivorous mind. Five times out of six the animal won. But when the mental prevailed, then there was an entrancing five minutes' digging among out-of-date almanacs, volumes of Scotch theology, and tables of logarithms, until one found something which made it all worth while. If you will look over these titles, you will see that I did not do so very badly. Four volumes of Gordon's "Tacitus" (life is too short to read originals so long as there are good translations), Sir William Temple's Essays, Addison's works, Swift's "Tale of a Tub," Clarendon's "History," "Gil Blas," Buckingham's Poems, Churchill's Poems, "Life of Bacon"—not so bad for the old threepenny tub.

They were not always in such plebeian company. Look at the thickness of the rich leather, and the richness of the dim gold lettering. Once they adorned the shelves of some noble library, and even among the odd almanacs and the sermons they bore the traces of their former greatness, like the faded silk dress of the reduced gentlewoman, a present pathos but a glory of the past.

Reading is made too easy nowadays, with cheap paper editions and free libraries. A man does not appreciate at its full worth the thing that comes to him without effort. Who now ever gets the thrill which Carlyle felt when he hurried home with the six volumes of Gibbon's "History" under his arm, his mind just starving for want of food, to devour them at the rate of one a day? A book should be your very own before you can really get the taste of it, and unless you have worked for it, you will never have the true inward pride of possession.

If I had to choose the one book out of all that line from which I have had most pleasure and most profit, I should point to yonder stained copy of Macaulay's "Essays." It seems entwined into my whole life as I look backwards. It was my comrade in my student days, it has been with me on the sweltering Gold Coast, and it formed part of my humble kit when I went a-whaling in the Arctic. Honest Scotch harpooners have addled their brains over it, and you may still see the grease stains where the second engineer grappled with Frederick the Great. Tattered and dirty and worn, no gilt-edged morocco-bound volume could ever take its place for me.

What a noble gateway this book forms through which one may approach the study either of letters or of history! Milton, Machiavelli, Hallam, Southey, Bunyan, Byron, Johnson, Pitt, Hampden, Clive, Hastings, Chatham—what nuclei for thought! With a good grip of each how pleasant and easy to fill in all that lies between. The short, vivid sentences, the broad sweep of allusion, the exact detail, they all throw a glamour round the subject and should make the least studious of readers desire to go further. If Macaulay's hand cannot lead a man upon those pleasant paths, then, indeed, he may give up all hope of ever finding them.

When I was a senior schoolboy this book —not this very volume, for it had an even more tattered predecessor—opened up a new world to me. History had been a lesson and abhorrent. Suddenly the task and the drudgery became an incursion into an enchanted land, a land of color and beauty, with a kind, wise guide to point the path. In that great style of his I loved even the faults—indeed, now that I come to think of it, it was the faults which I loved best. No sentence could be too stiff with rich embroidery, and no antithesis too flowery. It pleased me to read that "a universal shout of laughter from the Tagus to the Vistula informed the Pope that the days of the crusades were past," and I was delighted to learn that "Lady Jerningham kept a vase in which people placed foolish verses, and Mr. Dash wrote verses which were fit to be placed in Lady Jerningham's vase." Those were the kind of sentences which used to fill

me with a vague but enduring pleasure, like
chords which linger in the musician's ear. A
man likes a plainer literary diet as he grows
older, but still as I glance over the Essays I
am filled with admiration, and wonder at the
alternate power of handling a great subject,
and of adorning it by delightful detail—just
a bold sweep of the brush and then the most
delicate stippling. As he leads you down the
path, he for ever indicates the alluring side-
tracks which branch away from it. An admirable, if somewhat old-fashioned, literary
and historical education might be effected by
working through every book which is alluded
to in the Essays. I should be curious, however, to know the exact age of the youth when
he came to the end of his studies.

I wish Macaulay had written a historical
novel. I am convinced that it would have
been a great one. I do not know if he had
the power of drawing an imaginary character,
but he certainly had the gift of reconstruct-
ing a dead celebrity to a remarkable degree.

Look at the simple half-paragraph in which he gives us Johnson and his atmosphere. Was ever a more definite picture given in a shorter space—

"As we close it, the club-room is before us, and the table on which stand the omelet for Nugent, and the lemons for Johnson. There are assembled those heads which live for ever on the canvas of Reynolds. There are the spectacles of Burke, and the tall thin form of Langton, the courtly sneer of Beau-clerk and the beaming smile of Garrick, Gibbon tapping his snuff-box, and Sir Joshua with his trumpet in his ear. In the fore-ground is that strange figure which is as fa-miliar to us as the figures of those among whom we have been brought up—the gigantic body, the huge massy face, seamed with the scars of disease, the brown coat, the black worsted stockings, the gray wig with the scorched foretop, the dirty hands, the nails bitten and pared to the quick. We see the eyes and mouth moving with convulsive twitches; we see the heavy form rolling; we hear it puffing, and then comes the 'Why, sir!' and the 'What then, sir?' and the 'No, sir!' and the 'You don't see your way through the question, sir!'"

It is etched into your memory for ever.

I can remember that when I visited London at the age of sixteen the first thing I did after housing my luggage was to make a pilgrimage to Macaulay's grave where he lies in Westminster Abbey, just under the shadow of Addison, and amid the dust of the poets whom he had loved so well. It was the one great object of interest which London held for me. And so it might well be, when I think of all I owe him. It is not merely the knowledge and the stimulation of fresh interests, but it is the charming gentlemanly tone, the broad, liberal outlook, the general absence of bigotry and of prejudice. My judgment now confirms all that I felt for him then.

My four-volume edition of the History

stands, as you see, to the right of the Essays. Do you recollect the third chapter of that work—the one which reconstructs the England of the seventeenth century? It has always seemed to me the very high-water mark of Macaulay's powers, with its marvelous mixture of precise fact and romantic phrasing. The population of towns, the statistics of commerce, the prosaic facts of life are all transmuted into wonder and interest by the handling of the master. You feel that he could have cast a glamour over the multiplication table had he set himself to do so. Take a single concrete example of what I mean. The fact that a Londoner in the country, or a countryman in London, felt equally out of place in those days of difficult travel, would seem to hardly require stating, and to afford no opportunity of leaving a strong impression upon the reader's mind. See what Macaulay makes of it, though it is no more than a hundred other paragraphs which discuss a hundred various points—

"A cockney in a rural village, was stared at as much as if he had intruded into a kraal of Hottentots. On the other hand, when the lord of a Lincolnshire or Shropshire manor appeared in Fleet Street, he was as easily distinguished from the resident population as a Turk or a Lascar. His dress, his gait, his accent, the manner in which he gazed at the shops, stumbled into gutters, ran against the porters, and stood under the waterspouts, marked him out as an excellent subject for the operations of swindlers and banterers. Bullies jostled him into the kennel, Hackney coachmen splashed him from head to foot, thieves explored with perfect security the huge pockets of his horseman's coat, while he stood entranced by the splendor of the Lord Mayor's Show. Money-droppers, sore from the cart's tail, introduced themselves to him, and appeared to him the most honest friendly gentlemen that he had ever seen. Painted women, the refuse of Lewkner Lane and Whetstone Park, passed themselves on him for countesses and maids of honor. If he asked his way to St. James', his informants sent him to Mile End. If he went into a shop, he was instantly discerned to be a fit purchaser of everything that nobody else would buy, of second-hand embroidery, copper rings, and watches that would not go. If he rambled into any fashionable coffee-house, he became a mark for the insolent derision of fops, and the grave waggery of Templars. Enraged and mortified, he soon returned to his mansion, and there, in the homage of his tenants and the conversation of his boon companions, found consolation for the vexations and humiliations which he had undergone. There he was once more a great man, and saw nothing above himself except when at the assizes he took his seat on the bench near the Judge, or when at the muster of the militia he saluted the Lord Lieutenant."

On the whole, I should put this detached chapter of description at the very head of his

Essays, though it happens to occur in another volume.   The History as a whole does not, as it seems to me, reach the same level as the shorter articles.   One cannot but feel that it is a brilliant piece of special pleading from a fervid Whig, and that there must be more to be said for the other side than is there set forth, Some of the Essays are tinged also, no doubt, by his own political and religious limitations. The best are those which get right away into the broad fields of literature and philosophy. Johnson, Walpole, Madame D'Arblay, Addison, and the two great Indian ones, Clive and Warren Hastings, are my own favorites. Frederick the Great too, must surely stand in the first rank.   Only one would I wish to eliminate.   It is the diabolically clever criticism upon Montgomery.   One would have wished to think that Macaulay's heart was too kind, and his soul too gentle, to pen so bitter an attack.   Bad work will sink of its own weight. It is not necessary to souse the author as well. One would think more highly of the man if he had not done that savage bit of work.

I don't know why talking of Macaulay always makes me think of Scott, whose books, in a faded, olive-backed line, have a shelf, you see, of their own. Perhaps it is that they both had so great an influence, and woke such admiration in me. Or perhaps it is the real similarity in the minds and characters of the two men. You don't see it, you say? Well, just think of Scott's "Border Ballads," and then of Macaulay's "Lays." The machines must be alike, when the products are so similar. Each was the only man who could possibly have written the poems of the other. What swing and dash in both of them! What a love of all that is manly and noble and martial! So simple, and yet so strong. But there are minds on which strength and simplicity are thrown away. They think that unless a thing is obscure it must be superficial, whereas it is often the shallow stream which is turbid, and the deep which is clear. Do you remember the fatuous criticism of Matthew Arnold upon the glorious "Lays," where he calls out "Is this poetry?" after quoting—

> " And how can man die better
> Than facing fearful odds
> For the ashes of his fathers
> And the Temples of his Gods? "

In trying to show that Macaulay had not the poetic sense he was really showing that he himself had not the dramatic sense. The baldness of the idea and of the language had evidently offended him. But this is exactly where the true merit lies. Macaulay is giving the rough, blunt words with which a simple-minded soldier appeals to two comrades to help him in a deed of valor. Any high-flown sentiment would have been absolutely out of character. The lines are, I think, taken with their context, admirable ballad poetry, and have just the dramatic quality and sense which a ballad poet must have. That opinion of Arnold's shook my faith in his judgment, and yet I would forgive a good deal to the man who wrote—

" One more charge and then be dumb,
    When the forts of Folly fall,
May the victors when they come,
    Find my body near the wall."

Not a bad verse that for one's life aspiration.

This is one of the things which human society has not yet understood—the value of a
noble, inspiriting text.   When it does we shall
meet them everywhere engraved on appropriate places, and our progress through the
streets will be brightened and ennobled by one
continual series of beautiful mental impulses
and images, reflected into our souls from the
printed thoughts which meet our eyes.   To
think that we should walk with empty, listless
minds while all this splendid material is running to waste.   I do not mean mere Scrip-
tural texts, for they do not bear the same
meaning to all, though what human creature
can fail to be spurred onwards by "Work
while it is day, for the night cometh when no
man can work."   But I mean those beautiful
thoughts—who can say that they are uninspired thoughts?—which may be gathered

from a hundred authors to match a hundred uses. A fine thought in fine language is a most precious jewel, and should not be hid away, but be exposed for use and ornament. To take the nearest example, there is a horse-trough across the road from my house, a plain stone trough, and no man could pass it with any feelings save vague discontent at its ugliness. But suppose that on its front slab you print the verse of Coleridge—

> " He prayeth best who loveth best
> All things, both great and small,
> For the dear Lord who fashioned him
> He knows and loveth all."

I fear I may misquote, for I have not "The Ancient Mariner" at my elbow, but even as it stands does it not elevate the horse-trough? We all do this, I suppose, in a small way for ourselves. There are few men who have not some chosen quotations printed on their study mantelpieces, or, better still, in their hearts. Carlyle's transcription of "Rest! Rest! Shall I not have all Eternity to rest in!" is a pretty good spur to a weary man. But what we need is a more general application of the same thing for public and not for private use, until people understand that a graven thought is as beautiful an ornament as any graven image, striking through the eye right deep down into the soul.

However, all this has nothing to do with Macaulay's glorious lays, save that when you want some flowers of manliness and patriotism you can pluck quite a bouquet out of those. I had the good fortune to learn the Lay of Horatius off by heart when I was a child, and it stamped itself on my plastic mind, so that even now I can reel off almost the whole of it. Goldsmith said that in conversation he was like the man who had a thousand pounds in the bank, but could not compete with the man who had an actual sixpence in his pocket. So the ballad that you bear in your mind outweighs the whole bookshelf which waits for reference. But I want you now to move your eye a little farther down the shelf to the line of olive-green volumes. That is my edition of Scott. But surely I must give you a little breathing space before I venture upon them.

II

IT is a great thing to start life with a small number of really good books which are your very own. You may not appreciate them at first. You may pine for your novel of crude and unadulterated adventure. You may, and will, give it the preference when you can. But the dull days come, and the rainy days come, and always you are driven to fill up the chinks of your reading with the worthy books which wait so patiently for your notice. And then suddenly, on a day which marks an epoch in your life, you understand the difference. You see, like a flash, how the one stands for nothing and the other for literature. From that day onwards you may return to your crudities, but at least you do so with some standard of comparison in your mind. You can never be the same as you were be-

fore. Then gradually the good thing becomes more dear to you; it builds itself up
with your growing mind; it becomes a part of
your better self, and so, at last, you can look,
as I do now, at the old covers and love them
for all that they have meant in the past.   Yes,
it was the olive-green line of Scott's novels
which started me on to rhapsody.   They were
the first books I ever owned—long, long before I could appreciate or even understand
them.   But at last I realized what a treasure
they were.   In my boyhood I read them by
surreptitious candle-ends in the dead of the
night, when the sense of crime added a new
zest to the story.   Perhaps you have observed
that my "Ivanhoe" is of a different edition
from the others.   The first copy was left in
the grass by the side of a stream, fell into
the water, and was eventually picked up three
days later, swollen and decomposed, upon a
mud-bank.   I think I may say, however, that
I had worn it out before I lost it.   Indeed,
it was perhaps as well that it was some years

before it was replaced, for my instinct was always to read it again instead of breaking fresh ground.

I remember the late James Payn telling the anecdote that he and two literary friends agreed to write down what scene in fiction they thought the most dramatic, and that on examining the papers it was found that all three had chosen the same. It was the moment when the unknown knight, at Ashby-de-la-Zouch, riding past the pavilions of the lesser men, strikes with the sharp end of his lance, in a challenge to mortal combat, the shield of the formidable Templar. It was, indeed, a splendid moment! What matter that no Templar was allowed by the rules of his Order to take part in so secular and frivolous an affair as a tournament? It is the privilege of great masters to make things so, and it is a churlish thing to gainsay it. Was it not Wendell Holmes who described the prosaic man, who enters a drawing-room with a couple of facts, like ill-conditioned bull-dogs at his heels, ready to let them loose on any play of fancy? The great writer can never go wrong. If Shakespeare gives a sea-coast to Bohemia, or if Victor Hugo calls an English prize-fighter Mr. Jim-John-Jack—well, it *was* so, and that's an end of it. "There is no second line of rails at that point," said an editor to a minor author. "I make a second line," said the author; and he was within his rights, if he can carry his readers' conviction with him.

But this is a digression from "Ivanhoe." What a book it is! The second greatest historical novel in our language, I think. Every successive reading has deepened my admiration for it. Scott's soldiers are always as good as his women (with exceptions) are weak; but here, while the soldiers are at their very best, the romantic figure of Rebecca redeems the female side of the story from the usual commonplace routine. Scott drew manly men because he was a manly man himself, and found the task a sympathetic one.

He drew young heroines because a conven-

tion demanded it, which he had never the hard=
ihood to break.   It is only when we get him
for a dozen chapters on end with a minimum
of petticoat—in the long stretch, for example,
from the beginning of the Tournament to the
end of the Friar Tuck incident—that we realize the height of continued romantic narrative
to which he could attain.   I don't think in the
whole range of our literature we have a finer
sustained flight than that.

There is, I admit, an intolerable amount of
redundant verbiage in Scott's novels.   Those
endless and unnecessary introductions make
the shell very thick before you come to the
oyster.   They are often admirable in themselves, learned, witty, picturesque, but with no
relation or proportion to the story which they
are supposed to introduce.   Like so much of
our English fiction, they are very good matter
in a very bad place.   Digression and want of
method and order are traditional national sins.
Fancy introducing an essay on how to live on
nothing a year as Thackeray did in "Vanity

Fair," or sandwiching in a ghost story as Dickens has dared to do. As well might a dramatic author rush up to the footlights and begin telling anecdotes while his play was suspending its action and his characters waiting wearily behind him. It is all wrong, though every great name can be quoted in support of it. Our sense of form is lamentably lacking, and Sir Walter sinned with the rest. But get past all that to a crisis in the real story, and who finds the terse phrase, the short fire-word, so surely as he? Do you remember when the reckless Sergeant of Dragoons stands at last before the grim Puritan, upon whose head a price has been set: "A thousand marks or a bed of heather!" says he, as he draws. The Puritan draws also: "The Sword of the Lord and of Gideon!" says he. No verbiage there! But the very spirit of either man and of either party, in the few stern words, which haunt your mind. "Bows and Bills!" cry the Saxon Varangians, as the Moslem horse charges home. You feel it is

just what they must have cried. Even more
terse and businesslike was the actual battle-cry
of the fathers of the same men on that long-
drawn day when they fought under the "Red
Dragon of Wessex" on the low ridge at Hastings. "Out! Out!" they roared, as the Norman chivalry broke upon them. Terse,
strong, prosaic—the very genius of the race
was in the cry.

Is it that the higher emotions are not there?
Or is it that they are damped down and covered over as too precious to be exhibited?
Something of each, perhaps. I once met the
widow of the man who, as a young signal midshipman, had taken Nelson's famous messag∵
from the Signal Yeoman and communicated it
to the ship's company. The officers were impressed. The men were not. "Duty!" they
muttered. "We've always done it. Why
not?" Anything in the least high-falutin'
would depress, not exalt, a British company.
It is the under statement which delights them.
German troops can march to battle singing

Luther's hymns.   Frenchmen will work themselves into a frenzy by a song of glory and of Fatherland.   Our martial poets need not trouble to imitate—or at least need not imagine that if they do so they will ever supply a want to the British soldier.   Our sailors working the heavy guns in South Africa sang: "Here's another lump of sugar for the Bird." I saw a regiment go into action to the refrain of "A little bit off the top."   The martial poet aforesaid, unless he had the genius and the insight of a Kipling, would have wasted a good deal of ink before he had got down to such chants as these.   The Russians are not unlike us in this respect.   I remember reading of some column ascending a breach and singing lustily from start to finish, until a few survivors were left victorious upon the crest with the song still going.   A spectator inquired what wondrous chant it was which had warmed them to such a deed of valor, and he found that the exact meaning of the words, endlessly repeated, was "Ivan is in the garden picking cabbages." The fact is, I suppose, that a mere monotonous sound may take the place of the tom-tom of savage warfare, and hypnotize the soldier into valor.

Our cousins across the Atlantic have the same blending of the comic with their most serious work. Take the songs which they sang during the most bloody war which the Anglo-Celtic race has ever waged—the only war in which it could have been said that they were stretched to their uttermost and showed their true form—"Tramp, tramp, tramp," "John Brown's Body," "Marching through Georgia"—all had a playful humor running through them. Only one exception do I know, and that is the most tremendous war-song I can recall. Even an outsider in time of peace can hardly read it without emotion. I mean, of course, Julia Ward Howe's "War-Song of the Republic," with the choral opening line: "Mine eyes have seen the glory of the coming of the Lord." If that were ever sung upon a battlefield the effect must have been terrific.

A long digression, is it not? But that is the worst of the thoughts at the other side of the Magic Door. You can't pull one out without a dozen being entangled with it. But it was Scott's soldiers that I was talking of, and I was saying that there is nothing theatrical, no posing, no heroics (the thing of all others which the hero abominates), but just the short bluff word and the simple manly ways, with every expression and metaphor drawn from within his natural range of thought. What a pity it is that he, with his keen appreciation of the soldier, gave us so little of those soldiers who were his own contemporaries—the finest, perhaps, that the world has ever seen. It is true that he wrote a life of the great Soldier Emperor, but that was the one piece of hackwork of his career. How could a Tory patriot, whose whole training had been to look upon Napoleon as a malignant Demon, do justice to such a theme? But the Europe of those days was full of material which he of all men could have drawn with a sympathetic hand. What would we not give for a portrait of one of Murat's light-cavalrymen or of a Grenadier of the Old Guard, drawn with the same bold strokes as the Rittmeister of Gustavus or the archers of the French King's Guard in "Quentin Durward"?

In his visit to Paris Scott must have seen many of those iron men who during the preceding twenty years had been the scourge and also the redemption of Europe. To us the soldiers who scowled at him from the sidewalks in 1814 would have been as interesting and as much romantic figures of the past as the mail-clad knights or ruffling cavaliers of his novels. A picture from the life of a Peninsular veteran, with his views upon the Duke, would be as striking as Dugald Dalgetty from the German wars. But then no man ever does realize the true interest of the age in which he happens to live. All sense of proportion is lost, and the little thing hard-by obscures the great thing at a distance. It is easy in the dark to confuse the fire-fly and the star. Fancy, for example, the Old Masters seeking their subjects in inn parlors, or St. Sebastians, while Columbus was discovering America before their very faces.

I have said that I think "Ivanhoe" the best of Scott's novels. I suppose most people would subscribe to that. But how about the second best? It speaks well for their general average that there is hardly one among them which might not find some admirers who would vote it to a place of honor. To the Scottish-born man those novels which deal with Scottish life and character have a quality of raciness which gives them a place apart. There is a rich humor of the soil in such books as "Old Mortality," "The Antiquary," and "Rob Roy," which puts them in a different class from the others. His old Scottish women are, next to his soldiers, the best series of types that he has drawn. At the same time it must be admitted that merit which is associated with dialect has such limitations that it can never take the same place as work which makes an equal appeal to all the world. On the whole, perhaps, "Quentin Durward," on account of its wider interests, its strong character-drawing, and the European importance of the events and people described, would have my vote for the second place. It is the father of all those sword-and-cape novels which have formed so numerous an addition to the light literature of the last century. The pictures of Charles the Bold and of the unspeakable Louis are extraordinarily vivid. I can see those two deadly enemies watching the hounds chasing the herald, and clinging to each other in the convulsions of their cruel mirth, more clearly than most things which my eyes have actually rested upon.

The portrait of Louis with his astuteness, his cruelty, his superstition and his cowardice

is followed closely from Comines, and is the
more effective when set up against his bluff
and warlike rival. It is not often that
historical characters work out in their actual
physique exactly as one would picture them
to be, but in the High Church of Innsbruck
I have seen effigies of Louis and Charles
which might have walked from the very pages
of Scott—Louis, thin, ascetic, varminty; and
Charles with the head of a prize fighter. It
is hard on us when a portrait upsets all our
preconceived ideas, when, for example, we see
in the National Portrait Gallery a man with a
noble, olive-tinted, poetic face, and with a start
read beneath it that it is the wicked Judge
Jeffreys. Occasionally, however, as at Innsbruck, we are absolutely satisfied. I have before me on the mantelpiece yonder a portrait
of a painting which represents Queen Mary's
Bothwell. Take it down and look at it.
Mark the big head, fit to conceive large
schemes; the strong animal face, made to cap-
tivate a sensitive, feminine woman; the bru-

tally forceful features—the mouth with a suggestion of wild boars' tusks behind it, the beard which could bristle with fury: the whole man and his life-history are revealed in that picture. I wonder if Scott had ever seen the original which hangs at the Hepburn family seat?

Personally, I have always had a very high opinion of a novel which the critics have used somewhat harshly, and which came almost the last from his tired pen. I mean "Count Robert of Paris." I am convinced that if it had been the first, instead of the last, of the series it would have attracted as much attention as "Waverley." I can understand the state of mind of the expert, who cried out in mingled admiration and despair: "I have studied the conditions of Byzantine Society all my life, and here comes a Scotch lawyer who makes the whole thing clear to me in a flash!" Many men could draw with more or less success Norman England, or mediæval France, but to reconstruct a whole dead

civilization in so plausible a way, with such
dignity and such minuteness of detail, is, I
should think, a most wonderful *tour de force*.
His failing health showed itself before the end
of the novel, but had the latter half equaled
the first, and contained scenes of such
humor as Anna Comnena reading aloud her
father's exploits, or of such majesty as the
account of the muster of the Crusaders upon
the shores of the Bosphorus, then the book
could not have been gainsaid its rightful place
in the very front rank of the novels.

I would that he had carried on his narrative, and given us a glimpse of the actual
progress of the First Crusade. What an
incident! Was ever anything in the world's
history like it? It had what historical incidents seldom have, a definite beginning,
middle and end, from the half-crazed preach-
ing of Peter down to the Fall of Jerusalem.
Those leaders! It would take a second
Homer to do them justice. Godfrey the
perfect soldier and leader, Bohemund the un-

scrupulous and formidable, Tancred the ideal
knight errant, Robert of Normandy the half-
mad hero! Here is material so rich that one
feels one is not worthy to handle it. What
richest imagination could ever evolve anything
more marvelous and thrilling than the actual
historical facts?

But what a glorious brotherhood the novels
are! Think of the pure romance of "The
Talisman"; the exquisite picture of Hebridean
life in "The Pirate"; the splendid reproduction
of Elizabethan England in "Kenilworth";
the rich humor of the "Legend of Montrose";
above all, bear in mind that in all that splendid
series, written in a coarse age, there is not one
word to offend the most sensitive ear, and it
is borne in upon one how great and noble a
man was Walter Scott, and how high the service which he did for literature and for humanity.

For that reason his life is good reading, and
there it is on the same shelf as the novels.
Lockhart was, of course, his son-in-law and his

admiring friend.   The ideal biographer should be a perfectly impartial man, with a sympathetic mind, but a stern determination to tell the absolute truth.   One would like the frail, human side of a man as well as the other.   I cannot believe that any one in the world was ever quite so good as the subject of most of our biographies.   Surely these worthy people swore a little sometimes, or had a keen eye for a pretty face, or opened the second bottle when they would have done better to stop at the first, or did something to make us feel that they were men and brothers.   They need not go the length of the lady who began a biography of her deceased husband with the words— "D—— was a dirty man," but the books certainly would be more readable, and the subjects more lovable too, if we had greater light and shade in the picture.

But I am sure that the more one knew of Scott the more one would have admired him. He lived in a drinking age, and in a drinking country, and I have not a doubt that he took an allowance of toddy occasionally of an evening which would have laid his feeble successors under the table. His last years, at least, poor fellow, were abstemious enough, when he sipped his barley-water, while the others passed the decanter. But what a high-souled chivalrous gentleman he was, with how fine a sense of honor, translating itself not into empty phrases, but into years of labor and denial! You remember how he became sleeping partner in a printing house, and so involved himself in its failure. There was a legal, but very little moral, claim against him, and no one could have blamed him had he cleared the account by a bankruptcy, which would have enabled him to become a rich man again within a few years. Yet he took the whole burden upon himself and bore it for the rest of his life, spending his work, his time, and his health in the one long effort to save his honor from the shadow of a stain. It was nearly a hundred thousand pounds, I think, which he passed on to the creditors—a great

record, a hundred thousand pounds, with his
life thrown in.

And what a power of work he had! It was
superhuman. Only the man who has tried to
write fiction himself knows what it means
when it is recorded that Scott produced two
of his long novels in one single year. I remember reading in some book of reminiscences
—on second thoughts it was in Lockhart himself—how the writer had lodged in some rooms
in Castle Street, Edinburgh, and how he had
seen all evening the silhouette of a man out-
lined on the blind of the opposite house. All
evening the man wrote, and the observer could
see the shadow hand conveying the sheets of
paper from the desk to the pile at the side.
He went to a party and returned, but still the
hand was moving the sheets. Next morning
he was told that the rooms opposite were occupied by Walter Scott.

A curious glimpse into the psychology of
the writer of fiction is shown by the fact that
he wrote two of his books—good ones, too—

at a time when his health was such that he could not afterwards remember one word of them, and listened to them when they were read to him as if he were hearing the work of another man. Apparently the simplest processes of the brain, such as ordinary memory, were in complete abeyance, and yet the very highest and most complex faculty—imagination in its supreme form—was absolutely unimpaired. It is an extraordinary fact, and one to be pondered over. It gives some support to the feeling which every writer of imaginative work must have, that his supreme work comes to him in some strange way from without, and that he is only the medium for placing it upon the paper. The creative thought—the germ thought from which a larger growth is to come, flies through his brain like a bullet. He is surprised at his own idea, with no conscious sense of having originated it. And here we have a man, with all other brain functions paralyzed, producing this magnificent work. Is it possible that we are indeed but conduit pipes from the infinite reservoir of the unknown? Certainly it is always our best work which leaves the least sense of personal effort.

And to pursue this line of thought, is it possible that frail physical powers and an unstable nervous system, by keeping a man's materialism at its lowest, render him a more fitting agent for these spiritual uses? It is an old tag that

> "Great Genius is to madness close allied,
> And thin partitions do those rooms divide."

But, apart from genius, even a moderate faculty for imaginative work seems to me to weaken seriously the ties between the soul and the body.

Look at the British poets of a century ago: Chatterton, Burns, Shelley, Keats, Byron. Burns was the oldest of that brilliant band, yet Burns was only thirty-eight when he passed away, "burned out," as his brother terribly expressed it. Shelley, it is true, died by accident, and Chatterton by poison, but suicide is in itself a sign of a morbid state. It is true that Rogers lived to be almost a centenarian, but he was banker first and poet afterwards. Wordsworth, Tennyson, and Browning have all raised the average age of the poets, but for some reason the novelists, especially of late years, have a deplorable record. They will end by being scheduled with the white-lead workers and other dangerous trades. Look at the really shocking case of the young Americans, for example. What a band of promising young writers have in a few years been swept away! There was the author of that admirable book, "David Harum"; there was Frank Norris, a man who had in him, I think, the seeds of greatness more than almost any living writer. His "Pit" seemed to me one of the finest American novels. He also died a premature death. Then there was Stephen Crane—a man who had also done most brilliant work, and there was Harold Frederic, another master-craftsman. Is there any profession in the world which in proportion to its numbers could show such losses as that? In the meantime, out of our own men Robert Louis Stevenson is gone, and Henry Seton Merriman, and many another.

Even those great men who are usually spoken of as if they had rounded off their career were really premature in their end. Thackeray, for example, in spite of his snowy head, was only 52; Dickens attained the age of 58; on the whole, Sir Walter, with his 61 years of life, although he never wrote a novel until he was over 40, had, fortunately for the world, a longer working career than most of his brethren.

He employed his creative faculty for about twenty years, which is as much, I suppose, as Shakespeare did. The bard of Avon is another example of the limited tenure which Genius has of life, though I believe that he outlived the greater part of his own family, who were not a healthy stock. He died, I should judge, of some nervous disease; that is shown by the progressive degeneration of his signature. Probably it was locomotor ataxy, which is the special scourge of the imaginative man. Heine, Daudet, and how many more, were its victims. As to the tradition, first mentioned long after his death, that he died of a fever contracted from a drinking bout, it is absurd on the face of it, since no such fever is known to science. But a very moderate drinking bout would be extremely likely to bring a chronic nervous complaint to a disastrous end.

One other remark upon Scott before I pass on from that line of green volumes which has made me so digressive and so garrulous. No account of his character is complete which does not deal with the strange, secretive vein which ran through his nature. Not only did he stretch the truth on many occasions in order to conceal the fact that he was the author of the famous novels, but even intimate friends who met him day by day were not aware that he was the man about whom the whole of Europe was talking. Even his wife was ignorant of his pecuniary liabilities until the crash of the Ballantyne firm told her for the first time that they were sharers in the ruin. A psychologist might trace this strange twist of his mind in the numerous elfish Fenella-like characters who flit about and keep their irritating secret through the long chapters of so many of his novels.

It's a sad book, Lockhart's "Life." It leaves gloom in the mind. The sight of this weary giant, staggering along, burdened with debt, overladen with work, his wife dead, his nerves broken, and nothing intact but his honor, is one of the most moving in the history of literature. But they pass, these clouds, and all that is left is the memory of the supremely noble man, who would not be bent, but faced Fate to the last, and died in his tracks without a whimper. He sampled every human emotion. Great was his joy and great his success, great was his downfall and bitter his grief. But of all the sons of men I don't think there are many greater than he who lies under the great slab at Dryburgh.

III

WE can pass the long green ranks of the Waverley Novels and Lockhart's "Life" which flanks them. Here is heavier metal in the four big gray volumes beyond. They are an old-fashioned large-print edition of Boswell's "Life of Johnson." I emphasize the large print, for that is the weak point of most of the cheap editions of English Classics which come now into the market. With subjects which are in the least archaic or abstruse you need good clear type to help you on your way. The other is good neither for your eyes nor for your temper. Better pay a little more and have a book that is made for use.

That book interests me—fascinates me— and yet I wish I could join heartily in that chorus of praise which the kind-hearted old bully has enjoyed. It is difficult to follow his own advice and to "clear one's mind of cant" upon the subject, for when you have been accustomed to look at him through the sympathetic glasses of Macaulay or of Boswell, it is hard to take them off, to rub one's eyes, and to have a good honest stare on one's own account at the man's actual words, deeds, and limitations. If you try it you are left with the oddest mixture of impressions. How could one express it save that this is John Bull taken to literature—the exaggerated John Bull of the caricaturists—with every quality, good or evil, at its highest? Here are the rough crust over a kindly heart, the explosive temper, the arrogance, the insular narrowness, the want of sympathy and insight, the rudeness of perception, the positiveness, the overbearing bluster, the strong deep-seated religious principle, and every other characteristic of the cruder, rougher John Bull who was the great-grandfather of the present good-natured Johnnie.

If Boswell had not lived I wonder how much

we should hear now of his huge friend? With Scotch persistence he has succeeded in inoculating the whole world with his hero worship. It was most natural that he should himself admire him. The relations between the two men were delightful and reflect all credit upon each. But they are not a safe basis from which any third person could argue. When they met, Boswell was in his twenty-third and Johnson in his fifty-fourth year. The one was a keen young Scot with a mind which was reverent and impressionable. The other was a figure from a past generation with his fame already made. From the moment of meeting the one was bound to exercise an absolute ascendency over the other which made unbiased criticism far more difficult than it would be between ordinary father and son. Up to the end this was the unbroken relation between them.

It is all very well to pooh-pooh Boswell as Macaulay has done, but it is not by chance that a man writes the best biography in the language. He had some great and rare literary qualities. One was a clear and vivid style, more flexible and Saxon than that of his great model. Another was a remarkable discretion which hardly once permitted a fault of taste in this whole enormous book where he must have had to pick his steps with pitfalls on every side of him. They say that he was a fool and a coxcomb in private life. He is never so with a pen in his hand. Of all his numerous arguments with Johnson, where he ventured some little squeak of remonstrance, before the roaring "No, sir!" came to silence him, there are few in which his views were not, as experience proved, the wiser. On the question of slavery he was in the wrong. But I could quote from memory at least a dozen cases, including such vital subjects as the American Revolution, the Hanoverian Dynasty, Religious Toleration, and so on, where Boswell's views were those which survived.

But where he excels as a biographer is in telling you just those little things that you want to know. How often you read the life

of a man and are left without the remotest
idea of his personality. It is not so here.
The man lives again.   There is a short description of Johnson's person—it is not in the Life,
but in the Tour to the Hebrides, the very next
book upon the shelf, which is typical of his
vivid portraiture. May I take it down, and
read you a paragraph of it?—

"His person was large, robust, I may say
approaching to the gigantic, and grown un-
wieldy from corpulency. His countenance
was naturally of the cast of an ancient statue,
but somewhat disfigured by the scars of King's
evil. He was now in his sixty-fourth year
and was become a little dull of hearing. His
sight had always been somewhat weak, yet so
much does mind govern and even supply the
deficiencies of organs that his perceptions were
uncommonly quick and accurate. His head,
and sometimes also his body, shook with a kind
of motion like the effect of palsy. He appeared to be frequently disturbed by cramps
or convulsive contractions of the nature of that

distemper called St. Vitus' dance. He wore
a full suit of plain brown clothes, with twisted
hair buttons of the same color, a large bushy
grayish wig, a plain shirt, black worsted stockings and silver buckles. Upon this tour when
journeying he wore boots and a very wide
brown cloth great-coat with pockets which
might almost have held the two volumes of his
folio dictionary, and he carried in his hand a
large English oak stick." You must admit
that if one cannot reconstruct the great Samuel
after that it is not Mr. Boswell's fault—and
it is but one of a dozen equally vivid glimpses
which he gives us of his hero. It is just these
pen-pictures of his of the big, uncouth man,
with his grunts and his groans, his Gargan-
tuan appetite, his twenty cups of tea, and his
tricks with the orange-peel and the lamp-posts,
which fascinate the reader, and have given
Johnson a far broader literary vogue than his
writings could have done.

For, after all, which of those writings can
be said to have any life to-day? Not "Rasse-

las," surely—that stilted romance. "The Lives of the Poets" are but a succession of prefaces, and the "Ramblers" of ephemeral essays. There is the monstrous drudgery of the Dictionary, a huge piece of spadework, a monument to industry, but inconceivable to genius. "London" has a few vigorous lines, and the "Journey to the Hebrides" some spirited pages. This, with a number of political and other pamphlets, was the main output of his lifetime. Surely it must be admitted that it is not enough to justify his predominant place in English literature, and that we must turn to his humble, much-ridiculed biographer for the real explanation.

And then there was his talk. What was it which gave it such distinction? His clear-cut positiveness upon every subject. But this is a sign of a narrow finality—impossible to the man of sympathy and of imagination, who sees the other side of every question and understands what a little island the greatest human knowledge must be in the ocean of infinite possibilities which surround us. Look at the results. Did ever any single man, the very dullest of the race, stand convicted of so many incredible blunders? It recalls the remark of Bagehot, that if at any time the views of the most learned could be stamped upon the whole human race the result would be to propagate the most absurd errors. He was asked what became of swallows in the winter. Rolling and wheezing, the oracle answered: "Swallows," said he, "certainly sleep all the winter. A number of them conglobulate together by flying round and round, and then all in a heap throw themselves under water and lie in the bed of a river." Boswell gravely dockets the information. However, if I remember right, even so sound a naturalist as White of Selborne had his doubts about the swallows. More wonderful are Johnson's misjudgments of his fellow-authors. There, if anywhere, one would have expected to find a sense of proportion. Yet his conclusions would seem monstrous to a modern taste.

"Shakespeare," he said, "never wrote six consecutive good lines." He would only admit two good verses in Gray's exquisite " Elegy Written in a Country Churchyard," where it would take a very acid critic to find two bad ones. "Tristram Shandy" would not live. "Hamlet" was gabble. Swift's "Gulliver's Travels" was poor stuff, and he never wrote anything good except "A Tale of a Tub." Voltaire was illiterate. Rousseau was a scoundrel. Deists, like Hume, Priestley, or Gibbon, could not be honest men.

And his political opinions! They sound now like a caricature. I suppose even in those days they were reactionary. "A poor man has no honor." "Charles the Second was a good King." "Governments should turn out of the Civil Service all who were on the other side." "Judges in India should be encouraged to trade." "No country is the richer on account of trade." (I wonder if Adam Smith was in the company when this proposition was laid down!) "A landed proprietor should turn out those tenants who did not vote as he wished." "It is not good for a laborer to have his wages raised." "When the balance of trade is against a country, the margin *must* be paid in current coin." Those were a few of his convictions.

And then his prejudices! Most of us have some unreasoning aversion. In our more generous moments we are not proud of it. But consider those of Johnson! When they were all eliminated there was not so very much left. He hated Whigs. He disliked Scotsmen. He detested Nonconformists (a young lady who joined them was "an odious wench"). He loathed Americans. So he walked his narrow line, belching fire and fury at everything to the right or the left of it. Macaulay's posthumous admiration is all very well, but had they met in life Macaulay would have contrived to unite under one hat nearly everything that Johnson abominated.

It cannot be said that these prejudices were founded on any strong principle, or that they could not be altered where his own personal interests demanded it. This is one of the weak points of his record. In his dictionary he abused pensions and pensioners as a means by which the State imposed slavery upon hirelings. When he wrote the unfortunate definition a pension must have seemed a most improbable contingency, but when George III., either through policy or charity, offered him one a little later, he made no hesitation in accepting it. One would have liked to feel that the violent expression of his convictions represented a real intensity of feeling, but the facts in this instance seem against it.

He was a great talker—but his talk was more properly a monologue. It was a discursive essay, with perhaps a few marginal notes from his subdued audience. How could one talk on equal terms with a man who could not brook contradiction or even argument upon the most vital questions in life? Would Goldsmith defend his literary views, or Burke his Whiggism, or Gibbon his Deism? There

was no common ground of philosophic toleration on which one could stand. If he could
not argue he would be rude, or, as Goldsmith
put it: "If his pistol missed fire, he would
knock you down with the butt end." In the
face of that "rhinoceros laugh" there was an
end of gentle argument. Napoleon said that
all the other kings would say "Ouf!" when
they heard he was dead, and so I cannot help
thinking that the older men of Johnson's circle
must have given a sigh of relief when at last
they could speak freely on that which was near
their hearts, without the danger of a scene
where "Why, no, sir!" was very likely to ripen
into "Let us have no more on't!" Certainly
one would like to get behind Boswell's account,
and to hear a chat between such men as Burke
and Reynolds, as to the difference in the freedom and atmosphere of the Club on an evening when the formidable Doctor was not there,
as compared to one when he was.

No smallest estimate of his character is fair
which does not make due allowance for the

terrible experiences of his youth and early middle age. His spirit was as scarred as his face. He was fifty-three when the pension was given him, and up to then his existence had been spent in one constant struggle for the first necessities of life, for the daily meal and the nightly bed. He had seen his comrades of letters die of actual privation. From childhood he had known no happiness. The half blind gawky youth, with dirty linen and twitching limbs, had always, whether in the streets of Lichfield, the quadrangle of Pembroke, or the coffee-houses of London, been an object of mingled pity and amusement. With a proud and sensitive soul, every day of his life must have brought some bitter humiliation. Such an experience must either break a man's spirit or embitter it, and here, no doubt, was the secret of that roughness, that carelessness for the sensibilities of others, which caused Boswell's father to christen him "Ursa Major." If his nature was in any way warped, it must be admitted that terrific forces had gone to the

rending of it. His good was innate, his evil
the result of a dreadful experience.

And he had some great qualities. Memory
was the chief of them. He had read omniv-
orously, and all that he had read he remembered, not merely in the vague, general way
in which we remember what we read, but with
every particular of place and date. If it were
poetry, he could quote it by the page, Latin
or English. Such a memory has its enormous
advantage, but it carries with it its corre-
sponding defect. With the mind so crammed
with other people's goods, how can you have
room for any fresh manufactures of your
own? A great memory is, I think, often fatal
to originality, in spite of Scott and some other
exceptions. The slate must be clear before
you put your own writing upon it. When
did Johnson ever discover an original thought,
when did he ever reach forward into the future, or throw any fresh light upon those
enigmas with which mankind is faced? Over-
loaded with the past, he had space for nothing

else.   Modern developments of every sort cast
no first herald rays upon his mind.   He jour-
neyed in France a few years before the greatest cataclysm that the world has ever known,
and his mind, arrested by much that was trivial,
never once responded to the storm-signals
which must surely have been visible around
him.   We read that an amiable Monsieur
Sansterre showed him over his brewery and
supplied him with statistics as to his output of
beer.   It was the same foul-mouthed Sansterre
who struck up the drums to drown Louis' voice
at the scaffold.   The association shows how
near the unconscious sage was to the edge of
that precipice and how little his learning
availed him in discerning it.

He would have been a great lawyer or
divine.   Nothing, one would think, could have
kept him from Canterbury or from the Wool-
sack.   In either case his memory, his learning,
his dignity, and his inherent sense of piety and
justice, would have sent him straight to the
top.   His brain, working within its own limi-

tations, was remarkable. There is no more wonderful proof of this than his opinions on questions of Scotch law, as given to Boswell and as used by the latter before the Scotch judges. That an outsider with no special training should at short notice write such weighty opinions, crammed with argument and reason, is, I think, as remarkable a *tour de force* as literature can show.

Above all, he really was a very kind-hearted man, and that must count for much. His was a large charity, and it came from a small purse. The rooms of his house became a sort of harbor of refuge in which several strange battered hulks found their last moorings. There were the blind Mr. Levett, and the acidulous Mrs. Williams, and the colorless Mrs. De Moulins, all old and ailing—a trying group amid which to spend one's days. His guinea was always ready for the poor acquaintance, and no poet was so humble that he might not preface his book with a dedication whose ponderous and sonorous sentences bore the hallmark of their maker. It is the rough, kindly man, the man who bore the poor street-walker home upon his shoulders, who makes one forget, or at least forgive, the dogmatic pedantic Doctor of the Club.

There is always to me something of interest in the view which a great man takes of old age and death. It is the practical test of how far the philosophy of his life has been a sound one. Hume saw death afar, and met it with unostentatious calm. Johnson's mind flinched from that dread opponent. His letters and his talk during his latter years are one long cry of fear. It was not cowardice, for physically he was one of the most stout-hearted men that ever lived. There were no limits to his courage. It was spiritual diffidence, coupled with an actual belief in the possibilities of the other world, which a more humane and liberal theology has done something to soften. How strange to see him cling so desperately to that crazy body, with its gout, its asthma, its St. Vitus' dance, and its six gallons of dropsy!

What could be the attraction of an existence where eight hours of every day were spent groaning in a chair, and sixteen wheezing in a bed? "I would give one of these legs," said he, "for another year of life." None the less, when the hour did at last strike, no man could have borne himself with more simple dignity and courage. Say what you will of him, and resent him how you may, you can never open those four gray volumes without getting some mental stimulus, some desire for wider reading, some insight into human learning or character, which should leave you a better and a wiser man.

IV

NEXT to my Johnsoniana are my Gibbons—
two editions, if you please, for my old complete one being somewhat crabbed in the print
I could not resist getting a set of Bury's new
six-volume presentment of the History. In
reading that book you don't want to be handi-
capped in any way. You want fair type, clear
paper, and a light volume. You are not to
read it lightly, but with some earnestness of
purpose and keenness for knowledge, with a
classical atlas at your elbow and a note-book
hard by, taking easy stages and harking back
every now and then to keep your grip of the
past and to link it up with what follows.
There are no thrills in it. You won't be kept
out of your bed at night, nor will you forget
your appointments during the day, but you
will feel a certain sedate pleasure in the doing

of it, and when it is done you will have gained something which you can never lose—something solid, something definite, something that will make you broader and deeper than before.

Were I condemned to spend a year upon a desert island and allowed only one book for my companion, it is certainly that which I should choose. For consider how enormous is its scope, and what food for thought is contained within those volumes. It covers a thousand years of the world's history, it is full and good and accurate, its standpoint is broadly philosophic, its style dignified. With our more elastic methods we may consider his manner pompous, but he lived in an age when Johnson's turgid periods had corrupted our literature. For my own part I do not dislike Gibbon's pomposity. A paragraph should be measured and sonorous if it ventures to describe the advance of a Roman legion, or the debate of a Greek Senate. You are wafted upwards, with this lucid and just spirit by your side upholding and instructing you. Beneath you are warring nations, the clash of races, the rise and fall of dynasties, the conflict of creeds. Serene you float above them all, and ever as the panorama flows past, the weighty measured unemotional voice whispers the true meaning of the scene into your ear.

It is a most mighty story that is told. You begin with a description of the state of the Roman Empire when the early Cæsars were on the throne, and when it was undisputed mistress of the world. You pass down the line of the Emperors with their strange alternations of greatness and profligacy, descending occasionally to criminal lunacy. When the Empire went rotten it began at the top, and it took centuries to corrupt the man behind the spear. Neither did a religion of peace affect him much, for, in spite of the adoption of Christianity, Roman history was still written in blood. The new creed had only added a fresh cause of quarrel and violence to the many which already existed, and the wars of angry nations were mild compared to those of excited sectaries.

Then came the mighty rushing wind from without, blowing from the waste places of the world, destroying, confounding, whirling madly through the old order, leaving broken chaos behind it, but finally cleansing and purifying that which was stale and corrupt. A storm-center somewhere in the north of China did suddenly what it may very well do again. The human volcano blew its top off, and Europe was covered by the destructive *débris*. The absurd point is that it was not the conquerors who overran the Roman Empire, but it was the terrified fugitives who, like a drove of stampeded cattle, blundered over everything which barred their way. It was a wild, dramatic time—the time of the formation of the modern races of Europe. The nations came whirling in out of the north and east like dust-storms, and amid the seeming chaos each was blended with its neighbor so as to toughen the fiber of the whole. The fickle Gaul got his steadying from the Franks, the steady Saxon got his touch of refinement from the Norman, the Italian got a fresh lease of life from the Lombard and the Ostrogoth, the corrupt Greek made way for the manly and earnest Mahommedan. Everywhere one seems to see a great hand blending the seeds. And so one can now, save only that emigration has taken the place of war. It does not, for example, take much prophetic power to say that something very great is being built up on the other side of the Atlantic. When on an Anglo-Celtic basis you see the Italian, the Hun, and the Scandinavian being added, you feel that there is no human quality which may not be thereby evolved.

But to revert to Gibbon: the next stage is the flight of Empire from Rome to Byzantium, even as the Anglo-Celtic power might find its center some day not in London but in Chicago or Toronto. There is the whole strange story of the tidal wave of Mahommedanism from the south, submerging all

North Africa, spreading right and left to India on the one side and to Spain on the other, finally washing right over the walls of Byzantium until it, the bulwark of Christianity, became what it is now, the advanced European fortress of the Moslem. Such is the tremenduous narrative covering half the world's known history, which can all be acquired and made part of yourself by the aid of that humble atlas, pencil, and note-book already recommended.

When all is so interesting it is hard to pick examples, but to me there has always seemed to be something peculiarly impressive in the first entrance of a new race on to the stage of history. It has something of the glamour which hangs round the early youth of a great man. You remember how the Russians made their *début*—came down the great rivers and appeared at the Bosphorus in two hundred canoes, from which they endeavored to board the Imperial galleys. Singular that a thousand years have passed and that the ambition

of the Russians is still to carry out the task
at which their skin-clad ancestors failed. Or
the Turks again; you may recall the characteristic ferocity with which they opened their
career. A handful of them were on some mission to the Emperor. The town was besieged
from the landward side by the barbarians, and
the Asiatics obtained leave to take part in a
skirmish. The first Turk galloped out, shot
a barbarian with his arrow, and then, lying
down beside him, proceeded to suck his blood,
which so horrified the man's comrades that they
could not be brought to face such uncanny ad-
versaries. So, from opposite sides, those two
great races arrived at the city which was to be
the stronghold of the one and the ambition of
the other for so many centuries.

And then, even more interesting than the
races which arrive are those that disappear.
There is something there which appeals most
powerfully to the imagination. Take, for example, the fate of those Vandals who conquered the north of Africa. They were a

German tribe, blue-eyed and flaxen-haired, from somewhere in the Elbe country. Suddenly they, too, were seized with the strange wandering madness which was epidemic at the time. Away they went on the line of least resistance, which is always from north to south and from east to west. Southwest was the course of the Vandals—a course which must have been continued through pure love of adventure, since in the thousands of miles which they traversed there were many fair resting-places, if that were only their quest.

They crossed the south of France, conquered Spain, and, finally, the more adventurous passed over into Africa, where they occupied the old Roman province. For two or three generations they held it, much as the English hold India, and their numbers were at the least some hundreds of thousands. Presently the Roman Empire gave one of those flickers which showed that there was still some fire among the ashes. Belisarius landed in Africa and reconquered the province. The Vandals were cut off from the sea and fled inland. Whither did they carry those blue eyes and that flaxen hair? Were they exterminated by the negroes, or did they amalgamate with them? Travelers have brought back stories from the Mountains of the Moon of a Negroid race with light eyes and hair. Is it possible that here we have some trace of the vanished Germans?

It recalls the parallel case of the lost settlements in Greenland. That also has always seemed to me to be one of the most romantic questions in history—the more so, perhaps, as I have strained my eyes to see across the ice-floes the Greenland coast at the point (or near it) where the old "Eyrbyggia" must have stood. That was the Scandinavian city, founded by colonists from Iceland, which grew to be a considerable place, so much so that they sent to Denmark for a bishop. That would be in the fourteenth century. The bishop, coming out to his see, found that he was unable to reach it on account of a climatic change which had brought down the ice and filled the strait between Iceland and Greenland. From that day to this no one has been able to say what has become of these old Scandinavians, who were at the time, be it remembered, the most civilized and advanced race in Europe. They may have been overwhelmed by the Esquimaux, the despised Skroeling—or they may have amalgamated with them—or conceivably they might have held their own. Very little is known yet of that portion of the coast. It would be strange if some Nansen or Peary were to stumble upon the remains of the old colony, and find possibly in that antiseptic atmosphere a complete mummy of some bygone civilization.

But once more to return to Gibbon. What a mind it must have been which first planned, and then, with the incessant labor of twenty years, carried out that enormous work! There was no classical author so little known, no Byzantine historian so diffuse, no monkish chronicle so crabbed, that they were not assimi-

lated and worked into their appropriate place
in the huge framework. Great application,
great perseverance, great attention to detail
was needed in all this, but the coral polyp has
all those qualities, and somehow in the heart of
his own creation the individuality of the man
himself becomes as insignificant and as much
overlooked as that of the little creature that
builds the reef. A thousand know Gibbon's
work for one who cares anything for Gibbon.

And on the whole this is justified by the
facts. Some men are greater than their work.
Their work only represents one facet of their
character, and there may be a dozen others,
all remarkable, and uniting to make one complex and unique creature. It was not so with
Gibbon. He was a cold-blooded man, with a
brain which seemed to have grown at the expense of his heart. I cannot recall in his life
one generous impulse, one ardent enthusiasm,
save for the Classics. His excellent judgment
was never clouded by the haze of human emotion—or, at least, it was such an emotion as

was well under the control of his will. Could anything be more laudable—or less lovable? He abandons his girl at the order of his father, and sums it up that he "sighs as a lover but obeys as a son." The father dies, and he records the fact with the remark that "the tears of a son are seldom lasting." The terrible spectacle of the French Revolution excited in his mind only a feeling of self-pity because his retreat in Switzerland was invaded by the unhappy refugees, just as a grumpy country gentleman in England might complain that he was annoyed by the trippers. There is a touch of dislike in all the allusions which Boswell makes to Gibbon—often without even mentioning his name—and one cannot read the great historian's life without understanding why.

I should think that few men have been born with the material for self-sufficient contentment more completely within himself than Edward Gibbon. He had every gift which a great scholar should have, an insatiable thirst for learning in every form, immense industry, a retentive memory, and that broadly philosophic temperament which enables a man to rise above the partisan and to become the impartial critic of human affairs. It is true that at the time he was looked upon as bitterly prejudiced in the matter of religious thought, but his views are familiar to modern philosophy, and would shock no susceptibilities in these more liberal (and more virtuous) days. Turn him up in that Encyclopedia, and see what the latest word is upon his contentions. "Upon the famous fifteenth and sixteenth chapters it is not necessary to dwell," says the biographer, "because at this time of day no Christian apologist dreams of denying the substantial truth of any of the more important allegations of Gibbon. Christians may complain of the suppression of some circumstances which might influence the general result, and they must remonstrate against the unfair construction of their case. But they no longer refuse to hear any reasonable evi-

dence tending to show that persecution was
less severe than had been once believed, and
they have slowly learned that they can afford to
concede the validity of all the secondary causes
assigned by Gibbon and even of others still
more discreditable. The fact is, as the historian has again and again admitted, that his
account of the secondary causes which contrib-
uted to the progress and establishment of
Christianity leaves the question as to the natural or supernatural origin of Christianity
practically untouched." This is all very well,
but in that case how about the century of abuse
which has been showered upon the historian?
Some posthumous apology would seem to be
called for.

Physically, Gibbon was as small as Johnson was large, but there was a curious affinity
in their bodily ailments. Johnson, as a youth,
was ulcerated and tortured by the king's evil,
in spite of the Royal touch. Gibbon gives us
a concise but lurid account of his own boyhood.

"I was successively afflicted by lethargies and fevers, by opposite tendencies to a consumptive and dropsical habit, by a contraction of my nerves, a fistula in my eye, and the bite of a dog, most vehemently suspected of madness. Every practitioner was called to my aid, the fees of the doctors were swelled by the bills of the apothecaries and surgeons. There was a time when I swallowed more physic than food, and my body is still marked by the indelible scars of lancets, issues, and caustics."

Such is his melancholy report. The fact is that the England of that day seems to have been very full of that hereditary form of chronic ill-health which we call by the general name of struma. How far the hard-drinking habits in vogue for a century or so before had anything to do with it I cannot say, nor can I trace a connection between struma and learning; but one has only to compare this account of Gibbon with Johnson's nervous twitches, his scarred face and his St. Vitus' dance, to realize that these, the two most solid English writers of their generation, were each heir to the same gruesome inheritance.

I wonder if there is any picture extant of Gibbon in the character of subaltern in the South Hampshire Militia? With his small frame, his huge head, his round, chubby face, and the pretentious uniform, he must have looked a most extraordinary figure. Never was there so round a peg in a square hole! His father, a man of a very different type, held a commission, and this led to poor Gibbon becoming a soldier in spite of himself. War had broken out, the regiment was mustered, and the unfortunate student, to his own utter dismay, was kept under arms until the conclusion of hostilities. For three years he was divorced from his books, and loudly and bitterly did he resent it. The South Hampshire Militia never saw the enemy, which is perhaps as well for them. Even Gibbon himself pokes fun at them; but after three years under canvas it is probable that his men had more cause

to smile at their book-worm captain than he at
his men.   His hand closed much more readily
on a pen-handle than on a sword-hilt.   In his
lament, one of the items is that his colonel's example encouraged the daily practice of hard,
and even excessive drinking, which gave him
the gout.   "The loss of so many busy and idle
hours were not compensated for by any elegant
pleasure," says he; " and my temper was in-
sensibly soured by the society of rustic officers,
who were alike deficient in the knowledge of
scholars and the manners of gentlemen."
The picture of Gibbon flushed with wine at
the mess-table, with these hard-drinking
squires around him, must certainly have been
a curious one.   He admits, however, that he
found consolations as well as hardships in his
spell of soldiering.   It made him an Englishman once more, it improved his health, it
changed the current of his thoughts.   It was
even useful to him as an historian.   In a cele-
brated and characteristic sentence, he says,
"The discipline and evolutions of a modern

battalion gave me a clearer notion of the Phalanx and the Legions, and the captain of the Hampshire Grenadiers has not been useless to the historian of the Roman Empire."

If we don't know all about Gibbon it is not his fault, for he wrote no fewer than six accounts of his own career, each differing from the other, and all equally bad. A man must have more heart and soul than Gibbon to write a good autobiography. It is the most difficult of all human compositions, calling for a mixture of tact, discretion, and frankness which make an almost impossible blend. Gibbon, in spite of his foreign education, was a very typical Englishman in many ways, with the reticence, self-respect, and self-consciousness of the race. No British autobiography has ever been frank, and consequently no British autobiography has ever been good. Trollope's, perhaps, is as good as any that I know, but of all forms of literature it is the one least adapted to the national genius. You could not imagine a British Rousseau, still less a British

Benvenuto Cellini. In one way it is to the credit of the race that it should be so. If we do as much evil as our neighbors we at least have grace enough to be ashamed of it and to suppress its publication.

There on the left of Gibbon is my fine edition (Lord Braybrooke's) of Pepys' Diary. That is, in truth, the greatest autobiography in our language, and yet it was not deliberately written as such. When Mr. Pepys jotted down from day to day every quaint or mean thought which came into his head he would have been very much surprised had any one told him that he was doing a work quite unique in our literature. Yet his involuntary autobiography, compiled for some obscure reason or for private reference, but certainly never meant for publication, is as much the first in that line of literature as Boswell's book among biographies or Gibbon's among histories.

As a race we are too afraid of giving ourselves away ever to produce a good autobiography. We resent the charge of national hypocrisy, and yet of all nations we are the least frank as to our own emotions—especially on certain sides of them. Those affairs of the heart, for example, which are such an index to a man's character, and so profoundly modify his life—what space do they fill in any man's autobiography? Perhaps in Gibbon's case the omission matters little, for, save in the instance of his well-controlled passion for the future Madame Neckar, his heart was never an organ which gave him much trouble. The fact is that when the British author tells his own story he tries to make himself respectable, and the more respectable a man is the less interesting does he become. Rousseau may prove himself a maudlin degenerate. Cellini may stand self-convicted as an amorous ruffian. If they are not respectable they are thoroughly human and interesting all the same.

The wonderful thing about Mr. Pepys is that a man should succeed in making himself seem so insignificant when really he must have been a man of considerable character and at-

tainments. Who would guess it who read all
these trivial comments, these catalogues of
what he had for dinner, these inane domestic
confidences—all the more interesting for their
inanity! The effect left upon the mind is of
some grotesque character in a play, fussy, self-
conscious, blustering with women, timid with
men, dress-proud, purse-proud, trimming in
politics and in religion, a garrulous gossip im-
mersed always in trifles. And yet, though this
was the day-by-day man, the year-by-year man
was a very different person, a devoted civil
servant, an eloquent orator, an excellent writer,
a capable musician, and a ripe scholar who
accumulated 3,000 volumes—a large private
library in those days—and had the public spirit
to leave them all to his University. You can
forgive old Pepys a good deal of his philander-
ing when you remember that he was the only
official of the Navy Office who stuck to his post
during the worst days of the Plague. He may
have been—indeed, he assuredly was—a coward, but the coward who has sense of duty

enough to overcome his cowardice is the most truly brave of mankind.

But the one amazing thing which will never be explained about Pepys is what on earth induced him to go to the incredible labor of writing down in shorthand cipher not only all the trivialities of his life, but even his own very gross delinquencies which any other man would have been only too glad to forget. The Diary was kept for about ten years, and was abandoned because the strain upon his eyes of the crabbed shorthand was helping to destroy his sight. I suppose that he became so familiar with it that he wrote it and read it as easily as he did ordinary script. But even so, it was a huge labor to compile these books of strange manuscript. Was it an effort to leave some memorial of his own existence to single him out from all the countless sons of men? In such a case he would assuredly have left directions in somebody's care with a reference to it in the deed by which he bequeathed his library to Cambridge. In that way he could have en-

sured having his Diary read at any date he
chose to name after his death. But no allusion to it was left, and if it had not been for
the ingenuity and perseverance of a single
scholar the dusty volumes would still lie un-
read in some top shelf of the Pepysian
Library. Publicity, then, was not his object.
What could it have been? The only alterna-
tive is reference and self-information. You
will observe in his character a curious vein of
method and order by which he loved to be for
ever estimating his exact wealth, cataloguing
his books, or scheduling his possessions. It is
conceivable that this systematic recording of
his deeds—even of his misdeeds—was in some
sort analogous, sprung from a morbid tidiness
of mind. It may be a weak explanation but
it is difficult to advance another one.

One minor point which must strike the
reader of Pepys is how musical a nation the
English of that day appear to have been.
Every one seems to have had command of
some instrument, many of several. Part-

singing was common. There is not much of
Charles the Second's days which we need
envy, but there, at least, they seem to have
had the advantage of us. It was real music,
too—music of dignity and tenderness—with
words which were worthy of such treatment.
This cult may have been the last remains of
those mediæval pre-Reformation days when
the English Church choirs were, as I have read
somewhere, the most famous in Europe. A
strange thing this for a land which in the
whole of last century has produced no single
master of the first rank!

What national change is it which has
driven music from the land? Has life become so serious that song has passed out of
it? In Southern climes one hears poor folk
sing for pure lightness of heart. In England,
alas, the sound of a poor man's voice raised
in song means only too surely that he is drunk.
And yet it is consoling to know that the germ
of the old powers is always there ready to
sprout forth if they be nourished and culti-

vated. If our cathedral choirs were the best in the old Catholic days, it is equally true, I believe, that our orchestral associations are now the best in Europe. So, at least, the German papers said on the occasion of the recent visit of a north of England choir. But one cannot read Pepys without knowing that the general musical habit is much less cultivated now than of old.

V

It is a long jump from Samuel Pepys to George Borrow—from one pole of the human character to the other—and yet they are in contact on the shelf of my favorite authors. There is something wonderful, I think, about the land of Cornwall. That long peninsula extending out into the ocean has caught all sorts of strange floating things, and has held them there in isolation until they have woven themselves into the texture of the Cornish race. What is this strange strain which lurks down yonder and every now and then throws up a great man with singular un-English ways and features for all the world to marvel at? It is not Celtic, nor is it the dark old Iberian. Further and deeper lie the springs. Is it not Semitic, Phœnician, the roving men of Tyre, with noble Southern faces and Oriental imaginations, who have in far-off days forgotten their blue Mediterranean and settled on the granite shores of the Northern Sea?

Whence came the wonderful face and great personality of Henry Irving? How strong, how beautiful, how un-Saxon it was! I only know that his mother was a Cornish woman. Whence came the intense glowing imagination of the Brontës—so unlike the Miss-Austen-like calm of their predecessors? Again, I only know that their mother was a Cornish woman. Whence came this huge elfin creature, George Borrow, with his eagle head perched on his rocklike shoulders, brown-faced, white-headed, a king among men? Where did he get that remarkable face, those strange mental gifts, which place him by himself in literature? Once more, his father was a Cornishman. Yes, there is something strange, and weird, and great, lurking down yonder in the great peninsula which juts into the western sea. Borrow may, if he so pleases, call himself an East Anglian—"an English Englishman," as he loved to term it —but is it a coincidence that the one East Anglian born of Cornish blood was the one who showed these strange qualities? The birth was accidental. The qualities throw back to the twilight of the world.

There are some authors from whom I shrink because they are so voluminous that I feel that, do what I may, I can never hope to be well read in their works. Therefore, and very weakly, I avoid them altogether. There is Balzac, for example, with his hundred odd volumes. I am told that some of them are masterpieces and the rest pot-boilers, but that no one is agreed which is which. Such an author makes an undue claim upon the little span of mortal years. Because he asks too much one is inclined to give him nothing at all. Dumas, too! I stand on the edge of him, and look at that huge crop, and content myself with a sample here and there. But no one could raise this objection to Borrow.

A month's reading—even for a leisurely reader
—will master all that he has written. There
are "Lavengro," "The Bible in Spain,"
"Romany Rye," and, finally, if you wish to
go further, "Wild Wales." Only four books
—not much to found a great reputation upon
—but, then, there are no other four books
quite like them in the language.

He was a very strange man, bigoted, prejudiced, obstinate, inclined to be sulky, as way-
ward as a man could be. So far his catalogue
of qualities does not seem to pick him as a
winner. But he had one great and rare gift.
He preserved through all his days a sense of
the great wonder and mystery of life—the
child sense which is so quickly dulled. Not
only did he retain it himself, but he was word-
master enough to make other people hark back
to it also. As he writes you cannot help seeing through his eyes, and nothing which his
eyes saw or his ear heard was ever dull or commonplace. It was all strange, mystic, with
some deeper meaning struggling always to the

light. If he chronicled his conversation with
a washerwoman there was something arresting
in the words he said, something singular in her
reply. If he met a man in a public-house one
felt, after reading his account, that one
would wish to know more of that man. If
he approached a town he saw and made you
see—not a collection of commonplace houses
or frowsy streets, but something very strange
and wonderful, the winding river, the noble
bridge, the old castle, the shadows of the
dead. Every human being, every object, was
not so much a thing in itself, as a symbol and
reminder of the past. He looked through a
man at that which the man represented.
Was his name Welsh? Then in an instant
the individual is forgotten and he is off,
dragging you in his train, to ancient Britons,
intrusive Saxons, unheard-of bards, Owen
Glendower, mountain raiders and a thousand
fascinating things. Or is it a Danish name?
He leaves the individual in all his modern
commonplace while he flies off to huge skulls

at Hythe (in parenthesis I may remark that I have examined the said skulls with some care, and they seemed to me to be rather below the human average), to Vikings, Berserkers, Varangians, Harald Haardraada, and the innate wickedness of the Pope. To Borrow all roads lead to Rome.

But, my word, what English the fellow could write! What an organ-roll he could get into his sentences! How nervous and vital and vivid it all is!

There is music in every line of it if you have been blessed with an ear for the music of prose. Take the chapter in "Lavengro" of how the screaming horror came upon his spirit when he was encamped in the Dingle. The man who wrote that has caught the true mantle of Bunyan and Defoe. And, observe the art of it, under all the simplicity—notice, for example, the curious weird effect produced by the studied repetition of the word "dingle" coming ever round and round like the master-note in a chime. Or take the passage about

Britain towards the end of "The Bible in Spain." I hate quoting from these masterpieces, if only for the very selfish reason that my poor setting cannot afford to show up brilliants. None the less, cost what it may, let me transcribe that one noble piece of impassioned prose—

"O England! long, long may it be ere the sun of thy glory sink beneath the wave of darkness! Though gloomy and portentous clouds are now gathering rapidly around thee, still, still may it please the Almighty to disperse them, and to grant thee a futurity longer in duration and still brighter in renown than thy past! Or, if thy doom be at hand, may that doom be a noble one, and worthy of her who has been styled the Old Queen of the waters! May thou sink, if thou dost sink, amidst blood and flame, with a mighty noise, causing more than one nation to participate in thy downfall! Of all fates, may it please the Lord to preserve thee from a

disgraceful and a slow decay; becoming, ere
extinct, a scorn and a mockery for those self-
same foes who now, though they envy and
abhor thee, still fear thee, nay even against
their will, honor and respect thee. . . .
Remove from thee the false prophets, who
have seen vanity and divined lies; who have
daubed thy wall with untempered mortar, that
it may fall; who see visions of peace where
there is no peace; who have strengthened the
hands of the wicked, and made the heart of
the righteous sad. Oh, do this, and fear not
the result, for either shall thy end be a majestic and an enviable one; or God shall per-
petuate thy reign upon the waters, thou Old
Queen!"

Or take the fight with the Flaming Tin-
man.   It's too long for quotation—but read it,
read every word of it.   Where in the language
can you find a stronger, more condensed and
more restrained narrative?   I have seen with
my own eyes many a noble fight, more than

one international battle, where the best of two great countries have been pitted against each other—yet the second-hand impression of Borrow's description leaves a more vivid remembrance upon my mind than any of them. This is the real witchcraft of letters.

He was a great fighter himself. He has left a secure reputation in other than literary circles—circles which would have been amazed to learn that he was a writer of books. With his natural advantages, his six foot three of height and his staglike agility, he could hardly fail to be formidable. But he was a scientific sparrer as well, though he had, I have been told, a curious sprawling fashion of his own. And how his heart was in it—how he loved the fighting men! You remember his thumbnail sketches of his heroes. If you don't I must quote one, and if you do you will be glad to read it again—

"There's Cribb, the Champion of England, and perhaps the best man in England; there he is, with his huge, massive figure, and face wonderfully like that of a lion. There is Belcher, the younger, not the mighty one, who is gone to his place, but the Teucer Belcher, the most scientific pugilist that ever entered a ring, only wanting strength to be I won't say what. He appears to walk before me now, as he did that evening, with his white hat, white great-coat, thin genteel figure, springy step, and keen determined eye. Crosses him, what a contrast! Grim, savage Shelton, who has a civil word for nobody, and a hard blow for anybody. Hard! One blow given with the proper play of his athletic arm will unsense a giant. Yonder individual, who strolls about with his hands behind him, supporting his brown coat lappets, undersized, and who looks anything but what he is, is the king of the light-weights, so-called—Randall! The terrible Randall, who has Irish blood in his veins; not the better for that, nor the worse; and not far from him is his last antagonist, Ned Turner, who, though beaten by him, still thinks

himself as good a man, in which he is, perhaps, right, for it was a near thing. But how
shall I name them all? They were there by
dozens, and all tremendous in their way.
There was Bulldog Hudson, and fearless
Scroggins, who beat the conqueror of Sam the
Jew. There was Black Richmond—no, he
was not there, but I knew him well; he was the
most dangerous of blacks, even with a broken
thigh. There was Purcell, who could never
conquer until all seemed over with him. There
was—what! shall I name thee last? Ay, why
not? I believe that thou art the last of all that
strong family still above the sod, where mayst
thou long continue—true piece of English
stuff—Tom of Bedford. Hail to thee, Tom
of Bedford, or by whatever name it may please
thee to be called, Spring or Winter! Hail
to thee, six-foot Englishman of the brown
eye, worthy to have carried a six-foot bow at
Flodden, where England's yeomen triumphed
over Scotland's King, his clans and chivalry.
Hail to thee, last of English bruisers, after all

the many victories which thou hast achieved
—true English victories, unbought by yellow
gold."

Those are words from the heart. Long
may it be before we lose the fighting blood
which has come to us from of old! In a
world of peace we shall at last be able to root
it from our natures. In a world which is
armed to the teeth it is the last and only guar-
antee of our future. Neither our numbers,
nor our wealth, nor the waters which guard
us can hold us safe if once the old iron passes
from our spirit. Barbarous, perhaps—but
there are possibilities for barbarism, and none
in this wide world for effeminacy.

Borrow's views of literature and of literary
men were curious. Publisher and brother
author, he hated them with a fine comprehensive hatred. In all his books I cannot recall a word of commendation to any living
writer, nor has he posthumous praise for those
of the generation immediately preceding.

Southey, indeed, he commends with what most would regard as exaggerated warmth, but for the rest he who lived when Dickens, Thackeray, and Tennyson were all in their glorious prime, looks fixedly past them at some obscure Dane or forgotten Welshman. The reason was, I expect, that his proud soul was bitterly wounded by his own early failures and slow recognition. He knew himself to be a chief in the clan, and when the clan heeded him not he withdrew in haughty disdain. Look at his proud, sensitive face and you hold the key to his life.

Harking back and talking of pugilism, I recall an incident which gave me pleasure. A friend of mine read a pugilistic novel called "Rodney Stone" to a famous Australian prize-fighter, stretched upon a bed of mortal sickness. The dying gladiator listened with intent interest but keen, professional criticism to the combats of the novel. The reader had got to the point where the young amateur fights the brutal Berks. Berks is winded, but holds his adversary off with a stiff left arm. The amateur's second in the story, an old prize-fighter, shouts some advice to him as to how to deal with the situation. "That's right. By —— he's got him!" yelled the stricken man in the bed. Who cares for critics after that?

You can see my own devotion to the ring in that trio of brown volumes which stand, appropriately enough, upon the flank of Borrow. They are the three volumes of "Pugilistica," given me years ago by my old friend, Robert Barr, a mine in which you can never pick for half an hour without striking it rich. Alas! for the horrible slang of those days, the vapid, witless Corinthian talk, with its ogles and it fogles, its pointless jokes, its maddening habit of italicizing a word or two in every sentence. Even these stern and desperate encounters, fit sports for the men of Albuera and Waterloo, become dull and vulgar, in that dreadful jargon. You have to turn to Hazlitt's account of the encounter between the Gasman and the Bristol Bull, to feel the savage strength of it all. It is a hardened reader who does not wince even in print before that frightful right-hander which felled the giant, and left him in "red ruin" from eyebrow to jaw. But even if there be no Hazlitt present to describe such a combat it is a poor imagination which is not fired by the deeds of the humble heroes who lived once so vividly upon earth, and now only appeal to faithful ones in these little-read pages. They were picturesque creatures, men of great force of character and will, who reached the limits of human bravery and endurance. There is Jackson on the cover, gold upon brown, "gentleman Jackson," Jackson of the balustrade calf and the noble head, who wrote his name with an 88-pound weight dangling from his little finger.

Here is a pen-portrait of him by one who knew him well—

"I can see him now as I saw him in '84 walking down Holborn Hill, towards Smithfield. He had on a scarlet coat worked in gold at the buttonholes, ruffles and frill of fine lace, a small white stock, no collar (they were not then invented), a looped hat with a broad black band, buff knee-breeches and long silk strings, striped white silk stockings, pumps and paste buckles; his waistcoat was pale blue satin, sprigged with white. It was impossible to look on his fine ample chest, his noble shoulders, his waist (if anything too small), his large but not too large hips, his balustrade calf and beautifully turned but not over delicate ankle, his firm foot and peculiarly small hand, without thinking that nature had sent him on earth as a model. On he went at a good five miles and a half an hour, the envy of all men and the admiration of all women."

Now, that is a discriminating portrait—a portrait which really helps you to see that which the writer sets out to describe. After reading it one can understand why even in reminiscent sporting descriptions of those old days, amid all the Toms and Bills and Jacks, it is always Mr. John Jackson. He was the friend and instructor of Byron and of half the bloods in town. Jackson it was who, in the heat of combat, seized the Jew Mendoza by the hair, and so ensured that the pugs for ever afterwards should be a close-cropped race. Inside you see the square face of old Broughton, the supreme fighting man of the eighteenth century, the man whose humble ambition it was to begin with the pivot man of the Prussian Guard, and work his way through the regiment. He had a chronicler, the good Captain Godfrey, who has written some English which would take some beating. How about this passage?—

"He stops as regularly as the swordsman, and carries his blows truly in the line; he steps not back distrustful of himself, to stop a blow, and puddle in the return, with an arm unaided by his body, producing but flyflap blows. No! Broughton steps boldly and firmly in, bids a welcome to the coming blow; receives it with his guardian arm; then, with a general summons of his swelling muscles, and his firm body seconding his arm, and supplying it with all its weight, pours the pile-driving force upon his man."

One would like a little more from the gallant Captain. Poor Broughton! He fought once too often. "Why, damn you, you're beat!" cried the Royal Duke. "Not beat, your highness, but I can't see my man!" cried the blinded old hero. Alas, there is the tragedy of the ring as it is of life! The wave of youth surges ever upwards, and the wave that went before is swept sobbing on to the shingle. "Youth will be served," said the terse old pugs. But what so sad as the downfall of the old champion! Wise Tom Spring—Tom of Bedford, as Borrow calls him—had the wit to leave the ring unconquered in the prime of his fame. Cribb also stood out as a champion. But Broughton, Slack, Belcher, and the rest—their end was one common tragedy.

The latter days of the fighting men were often curious and unexpected, though as a rule they were short-lived, for the alternation of the excess of their normal existence and the asceticism of their training undermined their constitution. Their popularity among both men and women was their undoing, and the king of the ring went down at last before that deadliest of light-weights, the microbe of tubercle, or some equally fatal and perhaps less reputable bacillus. The crockiest of spectators had a better chance of life than the magnificent young athlete whom he had come to admire. Jem Belcher died at 30, Hooper at 31, Pearce, the Game Chicken, at 32, Turner at 35, Hudson at 38, Randall, the Nonpareil, at 34. Occasionally, when they did reach mature age, their lives took the strangest turns. Gully, as is well known, became a wealthy man, and Member for Pontefract in the Reform Parliament. Humphries developed into a successful coal merchant. Jack Martin be-

came a convinced teetotaller and vegetarian.
Jem Ward, the Black Diamond, developed
considerable powers as an artist. Cribb,
Spring, Langan, and many others, were successful publicans. Strangest of all, perhaps,
was Broughton, who spent his old age haunting every sale of old pictures and *bric-à-brac*.
One who saw him has recorded his impression
of the silent old gentleman, clad in old-fashioned garb, with his catalogue in his hand—
Broughton, once the terror of England, and
now the harmless and gentle collector.

Many of them, as was but natural, died
violent deaths, some by accident and a few
by their own hands. No man of the first
class ever died in the ring. The nearest approach to it was the singular and mournful
fate which befell Simon Byrne, the brave
Irishman, who had the misfortune to cause the
death of his antagonist, Angus Mackay, and
afterwards met his own end at the hands of
Deaf Burke. Neither Byrne nor Mackay
could, however, be said to be boxers of the

very first rank. It certainly would appear, if we may argue from the prize-ring, that the human machine becomes more delicate and is more sensitive to jar or shock. In the early days a fatal end to a fight was exceedingly rare. Gradually such tragedies became rather more common, until now even with the gloves they have shocked us by their frequency, and we feel that the rude play of our forefathers is indeed too rough for a more highly organized generation. Still, it may help us to clear our minds of cant if we remember that within two or three years the hunting-field and the steeple-chase claim more victims than the prize-ring has done in two centuries.

Many of these men had served their country well with that strength and courage which brought them fame. Cribb was, if I mistake not, in the Royal Navy. So was the terrible dwarf Scroggins, all chest and shoulders, whose springing hits for many a year carried all before them until the canny Welshman, Ned Turner, stopped his career, only to be stopped in turn by the brilliant Irishman, Jack Randall. Shaw, who stood high among the heavy-weights, was cut to pieces by the French Cuirassiers in the first charge at Waterloo. The brutal Berks died greatly in the breach of Badajos. The lives of these men stood for something, and that was just the one supreme thing which the times called for—an unflinching endurance which could bear up against a world in arms. Look at Jem Belcher—beautiful, heroic Jem, a manlier Byron—but there, this is not an essay on the old prize-ring, and one man's lore is another man's bore. Let us pass those three low-down, unjustifiable, fascinating volumes, and on to nobler topics beyond!

VI

Which are the great short stories of the English language? Not a bad basis for a debate! This I am sure of: that there are far fewer supremely good short stories than there are supremely good long books. It takes more exquisite skill to carve the cameo than the statue. But the strangest thing is that the two excellences seem to be separate and even antagonistic. Skill in the one by no means ensures skill in the other. The great masters of our literature, Fielding, Scott, Dickens, Thackeray, Reade, have left no single short story of outstanding merit behind them, with the possible exception of Wandering Willie's Tale in "Red Gauntlet." On the other hand, men who have been very great in the short story, Stevenson, Poe, and Bret Harte, have written no great book.   The champion sprinter is seldom a five-miler as well.

Well, now, if you had to choose your team whom would you put in?   You have not really a large choice.   What are the points by which you judge them?   You want strength, novelty, compactness, intensity of interest, a single vivid impression left upon the mind.   Poe is the master of all.   I may remark by the way that it is the sight of his green cover, the next in order upon my favorite shelf, which has started this train of thought.   Poe is, to my mind, the supreme original short story writer of all time.   His brain was like a seed-pod full of seeds which flew carelessly around, and from which have sprung nearly all our modern types of story.   Just think of what he did in his offhand, prodigal fashion, seldom troubling to repeat a success, but pushing on to some new achievement.   To him must be ascribed the monstrous progeny of writers on the detection of crime—*"quorum pars parva fui!"*   Each may find some little development of his own, but his main art must trace back to those admirable stories of Monsieur Dupin, so wonderful in their masterful force, their reticence, their quick dramatic point.   After all, mental acuteness is the one quality which can be ascribed to the ideal detective, and when that has once been admirably done, succeeding writers must necessarily be content for all time to follow in the same main track.   But not only is Poe the originator of the detective story; all treasure-hunting, cryptogram-solving yarns trace back to his "Gold Bug," just as all pseudo-scientific Verne-and-Wells stories have their prototypes in the "Voyage to the Moon," and the "Case of Monsieur Valdemar."   If every man who receives a cheque for a story which owes its springs to Poe were to pay tithe to a monument for the master, he would have a pyramid as big as that of Cheops.

And yet I could only give him two places in my team.   One would be for the "Gold Bug," the other for the "Murder in the Rue

Morgue." I do not see how either of those could be bettered. But I would not admit *perfect* excellence to any other of his stories. These two have a proportion and a perspective which are lacking in the others, the horror or weirdness of the idea intensified by the coolness of the narrator and of the principal actor, Dupin in the one case and Le Grand in the other. The same may be said of Bret Harte, also one of those great short story tellers who proved himself incapable of a longer flight. He was always like one of his own gold-miners who struck a rich pocket, but found no continuous reef. The pocket was, alas, a very limited one, but the gold was of the best. "The Luck of Roaring Camp" and "Tennessee's Partner" are both, I think, worthy of a place among my immortals. They are, it is true, so tinged with Dickens as to be almost parodies of the master, but they have a symmetry and satisfying completeness as short stories to which Dickens himself never at-

tained.   The man who can read those two stories without a gulp in the throat is not a man
I envy.

And Stevenson?   Surely he shall have two
places also, for where is a finer sense of what
the short story can do?   He wrote, in my
judgment, two masterpieces in his life, and
each of them is essentially a short story,
though the one happened to be published as
a volume.   The one is "Dr. Jekyll and Mr.
Hyde," which, whether you take it as a vivid
narrative or as a wonderfully deep and true
allegory, is a supremely fine bit of work.   The
other story of my choice would be "The
Pavilion on the Links"—the very model of
dramatic narrative.   That story stamped itself
so clearly on my brain when I read it in *Cornhill* that when I came across it again many
years afterwards in volume form, I was able
instantly to recognize two small modifications
of the text—each very much for the worse—
from the original form.   They were small
things, but they seemed somehow like a

chip on a perfect statue. Surely it is only a very fine work of art which could leave so definite an impression as that. Of course, there are a dozen other of his stories which would put the average writer's best work to shame, all with the strange Stevenson glamour upon them, of which I may discourse later, but only to those two would I be disposed to admit that complete excellence which would pass them into such a team as this.

And who else? If it be not an impertinence to mention a contemporary I should certainly have a brace from Rudyard Kipling. His power, his compression, his dramatic sense, his way of glowing suddenly into a vivid flame, all mark him as a great master. But which are we to choose from that long and varied collection, many of which have claims to the highest? Speaking from memory, I should say that the stories of his which have impressed me most are "The Drums of the Fore and Aft," "The Man who Would be King," "The Man who Was," and "The Brushwood Boy."

Perhaps, on the whole, it is the first two which I should choose to add to my list of master-pieces.

They are stories which invite criticism and yet defy it. The great batsman at cricket is the man who can play an unorthodox game, take every liberty which is denied to inferior players, and yet succeed brilliantly in the face of his disregard of law. So it is here. I should think the model of these stories is the most dangerous that any young writer could follow. There is digression, that most deadly fault in the short narrative; there is incoherence, there is want of proportion which makes the story stand still for pages and bound forward in a few sentences. But genius over-rides all that, just as the great cricketer hooks the off ball and glides the straight one to leg. There is a dash, an exuberance, a full-blooded, confident mastery which carries everything before it. Yes, no team of immortals would be complete which did not contain at least two representatives of Kipling.

And now whom? Nathaniel Hawthorne never appealed in the highest degree to me. The fault, I am sure, is my own, but I always seemed to crave stronger fare than he gave me. It was too subtle, too elusive, for effect. Indeed, I have been more affected by some of the short work of his son Julian, though I can quite understand the high artistic claims which the senior writer has, and the delicate charm of his style. There is Bulwer Lytton as a claimant. His "Haunted and the Haunters" is the very best ghost story that I know. As such I should include it in my list. There was a story, too, in one of the old *Blackwoods*—"Metempsychosis" it was called, which left so deep an impression upon my mind that I should be inclined, though it is many years since I read it, to number it with the best. Another story which has the characteristics of great work is Grant Allen's "John Creedy." So good a story upon so philosophic a basis deserves a place among the best. There is some first-class work to be picked also from

the contemporary work of Wells and of Quil-
ler-Couch which reaches a high standard.
One little sketch—"Old Œson" in "Noughts
and Crosses"—is, in my opinion, as good as
anything of the kind which I have ever read.

And all this didactic talk comes from looking at that old green cover of Poe. I am
sure that if I had to name the few books
which have really influenced my own life I
should have to put this one second only to
Macaulay's Essays. I read it young when my
mind was plastic. It stimulated my imagination and set before me a supreme example of
dignity and force in the methods of telling a
story. It is not altogether a healthy influence,
perhaps. It turns the thoughts too forcibly to
the morbid and the strange.

He was a saturnine creature, devoid of humor and geniality, with a love for the grotesque and the terrible. The reader must
himself furnish the counteracting qualities or
Poe may become a dangerous comrade. We
know along what perilous tracks and into what

deadly quagmires his strange mind led him, down to that gray October Sunday morning, when he was picked up, a dying man, on the sidewalk at Baltimore, at an age which should have seen him at the very prime of his strength and his manhood.

I have said that I look upon Poe as the world's supreme short story writer. His nearest rival, I should say, was Maupassant. The great Norman never rose to the extreme force and originality of the American, but he had a natural inherited power, an inborn instinct towards the right way of making his effects, which mark him as a great master. He produced stories because it was in him to do so, as naturally and as perfectly as an apple tree produces apples. What a fine, sensitive, artistic touch it is! How easily and delicately the points are made! How clear and nervous is his style, and how free from that redundancy which disfigures so much of our English work! He pares it down to the quick all the time.

I cannot write the name of Maupassant

without recalling what was either a spiritual interposition or an extraordinary coincidence in my own life. I had been traveling in Switzerland and had visited, among other places, that Gemmi Pass, where a huge cliff separates a French from a German canton. On the summit of this cliff was a small inn, where we broke our journey. It was explained to us that, although the inn was inhabited all the year round, still for about three months in winter it was utterly isolated, because it could at any time only be approached by winding paths on the mountain side, and when these became obliterated by snow it was impossible either to come up or to descend. They could see the lights in the valley beneath them, but were as lonely as if they lived in the moon. So curious a situation naturally appealed to one's imagination, and I speedily began to build up a short story in my own mind, depending upon a group of strong antagonistic characters being penned up in this inn, loathing each other and yet utterly unable

to get away from each other's society, every
day bringing them nearer to tragedy.   For a
week or so, as I traveled, I was turning over
the idea.

At the end of that time I returned through
France.   Having nothing to read I happened
to buy a volume of Maupassant's Tales which
I had never seen before.   The first story was
called "L'Auberge" (The Inn)—and as I ran
my eye down the printed page I was amazed
to see the two words, "Kandersteg" and
"Gemmi Pass."   I settled down and read it
with ever-growing amazement.   The scene
was laid in the inn I had visited.   The plot
depended on the isolation of a group of people through the snowfall.   Everything that I
imagined was there, save that Maupassant had
brought in a savage hound.

Of course, the genesis of the thing is clear
enough.   He had chanced to visit the inn, and
had been impressed as I had been by the same
train of thought.   All that is quite intelligible.
But what is perfectly marvelous is that in

that short journey I should have chanced to
buy the one book in all the world which would
prevent me from making a public fool of myself, for who would ever have believed that my
work was not an imitation? I do not think
that the hypothesis of coincidence can cover
the facts. It is one of several incidents in
my life which have convinced me of spiritual
interposition—of the promptings of some
beneficent force outside ourselves, which tries
to help us where it can. The old Catholic
doctrine of the Guardian Angel is not only a
beautiful one, but has in it, I believe, a real
basis of truth.

Or is it that our subliminal ego, to use the
jargon of the new psychology, or our astral, in
the terms of the new theology, can learn and
convey to the mind that which our own known
senses are unable to apprehend? But that is
too long a side track for us to turn down it.

When Maupassant chose he could run Poe
close in that domain of the strange and weird
which the American had made so entirely his

own. Have you read Maupassant's story called "La Horla"? That is as good a bit of *diablerie* as you could wish for. And the Frenchman has, of course, far the broader range. He has a keen sense of humor, breaking out beyond all decorum in some of his stories, but giving a pleasant sub-flavor to all of them. And yet, when all is said, who can doubt that the austere and dreadful American is far the greater and more original mind of the two?

Talking of weird American stories, have you ever read any of the works of Ambrose Bierce? I have one of his works there, "In the Midst of Life." This man had a flavor quite his own, and was a great artist in his way. It is not cheering reading, but it leaves its mark upon you, and that is the proof of good work.

I have often wondered where Poe got his style. There is a somber majesty about his best work, as if it were carved from polished jet, which is peculiarly his own. I dare say if

I took down that volume I could light anywhere upon a paragraph which would show
you what I mean.   This is the kind of thing—

"Now there are fine tales in the volumes
of the Magi—in the iron-bound melancholy
volumes of the Magi.   Therein, I say, are
glorious histories of the heaven and of the
earth, and of the mighty sea—and of the
genius that overruled the sea, and the earth,
and the lofty heaven.   There was much lore,
too, in the sayings which were said by the
Sybils, and holy, holy things were heard of
old·by the dim leaves which trembled round
Dodona, but as Allah liveth, that fable which
the Demon told me as he sat by my side in
the shadow of the tomb, I hold to be the most
wonderful of all."   Or this sentence: "And
then did we, the seven, start from our seats in
horror, and stand trembling and aghast, for
the tones in the voice of the shadow were not
the tones of any one being, but of a multitude
of beings, and, varying in their cadences from

syllable to syllable, fell duskily upon our ears in the well-remembered and familiar accents of many thousand departed friends."

Is there not a sense of austere dignity? No man invents a style. It always derives back from some influence, or, as is more usual, it is a compromise between several influences. I cannot trace Poe's. And yet if Hazlitt and De Quincey had set forth to tell weird stories they might have developed something of the kind.

Now, by your leave, we will pass on to my noble edition of "The Cloister and the Hearth," the next volume on the left.

I notice, in glancing over my rambling remarks, that I classed "Ivanhoe" as the second historical novel of the century. I dare say there are many who would give "Esmond" the first place, and I can quite understand their position, although it is not my own. I recognize the beauty of the style, the consistency of the character-drawing, the absolutely per-

fect Queen Anne atmosphere. There was
never an historical novel written by a man who
knew his period so thoroughly. But, great as
these virtues are, they are not the essential in
a novel. The essential in a novel is interest,
though Addison unkindly remarked that the
real essential was that the pastrycooks should
never run short of paper. Now "Esmond"
is, in my opinion, exceedingly interesting during the campaigns in the Lowlands, and when
our Machiavelian hero, the Duke, comes in, and
also whenever Lord Mohun shows his ill-
omened face; but there are long stretches of
the story which are heavy reading. A pre-
eminently good novel must always advance and
never mark time. "Ivanhoe" never halts for
an instant, and that just makes its superiority
as a novel over "Esmond," though as a piece
of literature I think the latter is the more perfect.

No, if I had three votes, I should plump
them all for "The Cloister and the Hearth,"
as being our greatest historical novel, and, in-

deed, as being our greatest novel of any sort.
I think I may claim to have read most of the
more famous foreign novels of last century,
and (speaking only for myself and within
the limits of my reading) I have been more
impressed by that book of Reade's and by Tol-
stoi's "Peace and War" than by any others.
They seem to me to stand at the very top of
the century's fiction.   There is a certain resem-
blance in the two—the sense of space, the number of figures, the way in which characters
drop in and drop out.   The Englishman is the
more romantic. . The Russian is the more real
and earnest.   But they are both great.

Think of what Reade does in that one book.
He takes the reader by the hand, and he leads
him away into the Middle Ages, and not a conventional study-built Middle Age, but a period
quivering with life, full of folk who are as
human and real as a 'bus-load in Oxford
Street.   He takes him through Holland, he
shows him the painters, the dykes, the life.   He
leads him down the long line of the Rhine, the

spinal marrow of Mediæval Europe. He shows him the dawn of printing, the beginnings of freedom, the life of the great mercantile cities of South Germany, the state of Italy, the artist-life of Rome, the monastic institutions on the eve of the Reformation. And all this between the covers of one book, so naturally introduced, too, and told with such vividness and spirit. Apart from the huge scope of it, the mere study of Gerard's own nature, his rise, his fall, his regeneration, the whole pitiable tragedy at the end, make the book a great one. It contains, I think, a blending of knowledge with imagination, which makes it stand alone in our literature. Let any one read the "Autobiography of Benvenuto Cellini," and then Charles Reade's picture of Mediæval Roman life, if he wishes to appreciate the way in which Reade has collected his rough ore and has then smelted it all down in his fiery imagination. It is a good thing to have the industry to collect facts. It is a greater and a rarer one to have the tact to know how to use them when you have got them. To be exact without pedantry, and thorough without being dull, that should be the ideal of the writer of historical romance.

Reade is one of the most perplexing figures in our literature. Never was there a man so hard to place. At his best he is the best we have. At his worst he is below the level of Surreyside melodrama. But his best have weak pieces, and his worst have good. There is always silk among his cotton, and cotton among his silk. But, for all his flaws, the man who, in addition to the great book of which I have already spoken, wrote "It is Never Too Late to Mend," "Hard Cash," "Foul Play," and "Griffith Gaunt," must always stand in the very first rank of our novelists.

There is a quality of heart about his work which I recognize nowhere else. He so absolutely loves his own heroes and heroines, while he so cordially detests his own villains, that he sweeps your emotions along with his own. No one has ever spoken warmly enough of the humanity and the lovability of his women. It is a rare gift—very rare for a man—this power of drawing a human and delightful girl. If there is a better one in nineteenth-century fiction than Julia Dodd I have never had the pleasure of meeting her. A man who could draw a character so delicate and so delightful, and yet could write such an episode as that of the Robber Inn in "The Cloister and the Hearth," adventurous romance in its highest form, has such a range of power as is granted to few men. My hat is always ready to come off to Charles Reade.

VII

It is good to have the magic door shut behind us. On the other side of that door are the world and its troubles, hopes and fears, headaches and heartaches, ambitions and disappointments; but within, as you lie back on the green settee, and face the long lines of your silent soothing comrades, there is only peace of spirit and rest of mind in the company of the great dead. Learn to love, learn to admire them; learn to know what their comradeship means; for until you have done so the greatest solace and anodyne God has given man have not yet shed their blessing upon you. Here behind this magic door is the rest house, where you may forget the past, enjoy the present, and prepare for the future.

You who have sat with me before upon the green settee are familiar with the upper shelf, with the tattered Macaulay, the dapper Gibbon, the drab Boswell, the olive-green Scott, the pied Borrow, and all the goodly company who rub shoulders yonder. By the way, how one wishes that one's dear friends would only be friends also with each other. Why should Borrow snarl so churlishly at Scott? One would have thought that noble spirit and romantic fancy would have charmed the huge vagrant, and yet there is no word too bitter for the younger man to use towards the elder. The fact is that Borrow had one dangerous virus in him—a poison which distorts the whole vision—for he was a bigoted sectarian in religion, seeing no virtue outside his own interpretation of the great riddle. Downright heathendom, the blood-stained Berserk or the chanting Druid, appealed to his mind through his imagination, but the man of his own creed and time who differed from him in minutiæ of ritual, or in the interpretation of mystic passages, was at once evil to the bone, and he had no charity of any sort for such a

person.   Scott therefore, with his reverent regard for old usages, became at once hateful
in his eyes.   In any case he was a disap-
pointed man, the big Borrow, and I cannot
remember that he ever had much to say that
was good of any brother author.   Only in the
bards of Wales and in the Scalds of the Sagas
did he seem to find his kindred spirits, though
it has been suggested that his complex nature
took this means of informing the world that he
could read both Cymric and Norse.   But we
must not be unkind behind the magic door—
and yet to be charitable to the uncharitable is
surely the crown of virtue.

So much for the top line, concerning which
I have already gossiped for six sittings, but
there is no surcease for you, reader, for as you
see there is a second line, and yet a third, all
equally dear to my heart, and all appealing in
the same degree to my emotions and to my
memory.   Be as patient as you may, while I
talk of these old friends, and tell you why I
love them, and all that they have meant to me

in the past. If you picked any book from that line you would be picking a little fiber also from my mind, very small, no doubt, and yet an intimate and essential part of what is now myself. Hereditary impulses, personal experiences, books—those are the three forces which go to the making of man. These are the books.

This second line consists, as you see, of novelists of the eighteenth century, or those of them whom I regard as essential. After all, putting aside single books, such as Sterne's "Tristram Shandy," Goldsmith's "Vicar of Wakefield," and Miss Burney's "Evelina," there are only three authors who count, and they in turn wrote only three books each, of first-rate importance, so that by the mastery of nine books one might claim to have a fairly broad view of this most important and distinctive branch of English literature. The three men are, of course, Fielding, Richardson, and Smollett. The books are: Richardson's "Clarissa Harlowe," "Pamela," and "Sir

Charles Grandison"; Fielding's "Tom Jones," "Joseph Andrews," and "Amelia"; Smollett's "Peregrine Pickle," "Humphrey Clinker," and "Roderick Random." There we have the real work of the three great contemporaries who illuminated the middle of the eighteenth century—only nine volumes in all. Let us walk around these nine volumes, therefore, and see whether we cannot discriminate and throw a little light, after this interval of a hundred and fifty years, upon their comparative aims, and how far they have justified them by the permanent value of their work. A fat little bookseller in the City, a rakehell wit of noble blood, and a rugged Scotch surgeon from the navy—those are the three strange immortals who now challenge a comparison— the three men who dominate the fiction of their century, and to whom we owe it that the life and the types of that century are familiar to us, their fifth generation.

It is not a subject to be dogmatic upon, for I can imagine that these three writers would appeal quite differently to every temperament, and that whichever one might desire to champion one could find arguments to sustain one's choice. Yet I cannot think that any large section of the critical public could maintain that Smollett was on the same level as the other two. Ethically he is gross, though his grossness is accompanied by a full-blooded humor which is more mirth-compelling than the more polished wit of his rivals. I can remember in callow boyhood—*puris omnia pura*—reading "Peregrine Pickle," and laughing until I cried over the Banquet in the Fashion of the Ancients. I read it again in my manhood with the same effect, though with a greater appreciation of its inherent bestiality. That merit, a gross primitive merit, he has in a high degree, but in no other respect can he challenge comparison with either Fielding or Richardson. His view of life is far more limited, his characters less varied, his incidents less distinctive, and his thoughts less deep.   Assuredly I, for one, should award him the third place in the trio.

But how about Richardson and Fielding? There is indeed a competition of giants.   Let us take the points of each in turn, and then compare them with each other.

There is one characteristic, the rarest and subtlest of all, which each of them had in a supreme degree.   Each could draw the most delightful women—the most perfect women, I think, in the whole range of our literature. If the eighteenth-century women were like that, then the eighteenth-century men got a great deal more than they ever deserved. They had such a charming little dignity of their own, such good sense, and yet such dear, pretty, dainty ways, so human and so charming, that even now they become our ideals. One cannot come to know them without a double emotion, one of respectful devotion towards themselves, and the other of abhorrence for the herd of swine who surrounded them.

Pamela, Harriet Byron, Clarissa, Amelia, and
Sophia Western were all equally delightful,
and it was not the negative charm of the inno-
cent and colorless woman, the amiable doll of
the nineteenth century, but it was a beauty of
nature depending upon an alert mind, clear
and strong principles, true womanly feelings,
and complete feminine charm.   In this respect
our rival authors may claim a tie; for I could
not give a preference to one set of these perfect creatures over another.   The plump little
printer and the worn-out man-about-town had
each a supreme woman in his mind.

But their men!   Alas, what a drop is there!
To say that we are all capable of doing what
Tom Jones did— as I have seen stated—is the
worst form of inverted cant, the cant which
makes us out worse than we are.   It is a libel
on mankind to say that a man who truly loves
a woman is usually false to her, and, above
all, a libel that he should be false in the vile
fashion which aroused good Tom Newcome's
indignation.   Tom Jones was no more fit to

touch the hem of Sophia's dress than Captain
Booth was to be the mate of Amelia. Never
once has Fielding drawn a gentleman, save
perhaps Squire Alworthy. A lusty, brawling,
good-hearted, material creature was the best
that he could fashion. Where, in his heroes,
is there one touch of distinction, of spiritual-
ity, of nobility? Here I think that the plebeian printer has done very much better than
the aristocrat. Sir Charles Grandison is a
very noble type—spoiled a little by over-cod-
dling on the part of his creator perhaps, but
a very high-souled and exquisite gentleman
all the same. Had *he* married Sophia or
Amelia I should not have forbidden the banns.
Even the persevering Mr. B—— and the too
amorous Lovelace were, in spite of their ab-
errations, men of gentle nature, and had possibilities of greatness and tenderness within
them. Yes, I cannot doubt that Richardson
drew the higher type of man—and that in
Grandison he has done what has seldom or
never been bettered.

Richardson was also the subtler and deeper writer in my opinion. He concerns himself with fine consistent character-drawing, and with a very searching analysis of the human heart, which is done so easily, and in such simple English, that the depth and truth of it only come upon reflection. He condescends to none of those scuffles and buffetings and pantomime rallies which enliven, but cheapen, many of Fielding's pages. The latter has, it may be granted, a broader view of life. He had personal acquaintance of circles far above, and also far below, any which the douce citizen, who was his rival, had ever been able or willing to explore. His pictures of low London life, the prison scenes in "Amelia," the thieves' kitchens in "Jonathan Wild," the sponging houses and the slums are as vivid and as complete as those of his friend Hogarth— the most British of artists, even as Fielding was the most British of writers. But the greatest and most permanent facts of life are to be found in the smallest circles. Two men and a woman may furnish either the tragedian or the comedian with the most satisfying theme.   And so, although his range was limited, Richardson knew very clearly and very thoroughly just that knowledge which was essential for his purpose.   Pamela, the perfect woman of humble life, Clarissa the perfect lady, Grandison the ideal gentleman—these were the three figures on which he lavished his most loving art.   And now, after one hundred and fifty years, I do not know where we may find more satisfying types.

He was prolix, it may be admitted, but who could bear to have him cut?   He loved to sit down and tell you just all about it.   His use of letters for his narratives made this gossipy style more easy.   First *he* writes and he tells all that passed.   You have his letter. *She* at the same time writes to her friend, and also states her views.   This also you see. The friends in each case reply, and you have the advantage of their comments and advice. You really do know all about it before you finish.   It may be a little wearisome at first, if you have been accustomed to a more hustling style with fireworks in every chapter. But gradually it creates an atmosphere in which you live, and you come to know these people, with their characters and their troubles, as you know no others of the dream-folk fiction.   Three times as long as an ordinary book no doubt, but why grudge the time?   What is the hurry.   Surely it is better to read one masterpiece than three books which will leave no permanent impression on the mind.

It was all attuned to the sedate life of that, the last of the quiet centuries.   In the lonely country-house, with few letters and fewer papers, do you suppose that the readers ever complained of the length of a book, or could have too much of the happy Pamela or of the unhappy Clarissa?   It is only under extraordinary circumstances that one can now get into that receptive frame of mind which was normal then.   Such an occasion is recorded by

Macaulay, when he tells how in some Indian hill station, where books were rare, he let loose a copy of "Clarissa." The effect was what might have been expected. Richardson in a suitable environment went through the community like a mild fever. They lived him, and dreamed him, until the whole episode passed into literary history, never to be forgotten by those who experienced it. It is tuned for every ear. That beautiful style is so correct and yet so simple that there is no page which a scholar may not applaud nor a servant-maid understand.

Of course, there are obvious disadvantages to the tale which is told in letters. Scott reverted to it in "Guy Mannering," and there are other conspicuous successes, but vividness is always gained at the expense of a strain upon the reader's good-nature and credulity. One feels that these constant details, these long conversations, could not possibly have been recorded in such a fashion. The indignant and dishevelled heroine could not sit down and record her escape with such cool minuteness of description. Richardson does it as well as it could be done, but it remains intrinsically faulty. Fielding, using the third person, broke all the fetters which bound his rival, and gave a freedom and personal authority to the novel which it had never before enjoyed. There at least he is the master.

And yet, on the whole, my balance inclines towards Richardson, though I dare say I am one in a hundred in thinking so. First of all, beyond anything I may have already urged, he had the supreme credit of having been the first. Surely the originator should have a higher place than the imitator, even if in imitating he should also improve and amplify. It is Richardson and not Fielding who is the father of the English novel, the man who first saw that without romantic gallantry, and without bizarre imaginings, enthralling stories may be made from everyday life, told in everyday language. This was his great new departure. So entirely was Field-

ing his imitator, or rather perhaps his paro-
dist, that with supreme audacity (some would
say brazen impudence) he used poor Richardson's own characters, taken from "Pamela"
in his own first novel, "Joseph Andrews," and
used them too for the unkind purpose of rid-
iculing them. As a matter of literary ethics,
it is as if Thackeray wrote a novel bringing in
Pickwick and Sam Weller in order to show
what faulty characters these were. It is no
wonder that even the gentle little printer grew
wrath, and alluded to his rival as a somewhat
unscrupulous man.

And then there is the vexed question of
morals. Surely in talking of this also, there
is a good deal of inverted cant among a certain class of critics. The inference appears
to be that there is some subtle connection between immorality and art, as if the handling
of the lewd, or the depicting of it, were in
some sort the hallmark of the true artist. It
is not difficult to handle or depict. On the
contrary, it is so easy, and so essentially dra-

matic in many of its forms, that the temptation to employ it is ever present. It is the easiest and cheapest of all methods of creating a spurious effect. The difficulty does not lie in doing it. The difficulty lies in avoiding it. But one tries to avoid it because on the face of it there is no reason why a writer should cease to be a gentleman, or that he should write for a woman's eyes that which he would be justly knocked down for having said in a woman's ears. But "you must draw the world as it is." Why must you? Surely it is just in selection and restraint that the artist is shown. It is true that in a coarser age great writers heeded no restrictions, but life itself had fewer restrictions then. We are of our own age, and must live up to it.

But must these sides of life be absolutely excluded? By no means. Our decency need not weaken into prudery. It all lies in the spirit in which it is done. No one who wished to lecture on these various spirits could preach on a better text than these three great rivals,

Richardson, Fielding, and Smollett. It is possible to draw vice with some freedom for the purpose of condemning it. Such a writer is a moralist, and there is no better example than Richardson. Again, it is possible to draw vice with neither sympathy nor disapprobation, but simply as a fact which is there. Such a writer is a realist, and such was Fielding. Once more, it is possible to draw vice in order to extract amusement from it. Such a man is a coarse humorist, and such was Smollett. Lastly, it is possible to draw vice in order to show sympathy with it. Such a man is a wicked man, and there were many among the writers of the Restoration. But of all reasons that exist for treating this side of life, Richardson's were the best, and nowhere do we find it more deftly done.

Apart from his writings, there must have been something very noble about Fielding as a man. He was a better hero than any that he drew. Alone he accepted the task of cleansing London, at that time the most dangerous and lawless of European capitals. Hogarth's pictures give some notion of it in the pre-Fielding day, the low roughs, the high-born bullies, the drunkenness, the villainies, the thieves' kitchens with their riverside trapdoors, down which the body is thrust. This was the Augean stable which had to be cleaned, and poor Hercules was weak and frail and physically more fitted for a sick-room than for such a task. It cost him his life, for he died at 47, worn out with his own exertions. It might well have cost him his life in more dramatic fashion, for he had become a marked man to the criminal classes, and he headed his own search-parties, when, on the information of some bribed rascal, a new den of villainy was exposed. But he carried his point. In little more than a year the thing was done, and London turned from the most rowdy to what it has ever since remained, the most law-abiding of European capitals. Has any man ever left a finer monument behind him?

If you want the real human Fielding you

will find him not in the novels, where his real
kindliness is too often veiled by a mock cyni-
cism, but in his "Diary of his Voyage to Lis-
bon." He knew that his health was irretriev-
ably ruined and that his years were numbered.
Those are the days when one sees a man as he
is, when he has no longer a motive for affectation or pretense in the immediate presence of
the most tremendous of all realities. Yet, sitting in the shadow of death, Fielding dis-
played a quiet, gentle courage and constancy
of mind, which show how splendid a nature
had been shrouded by his earlier frailties.

Just one word upon another eighteenth-century novel before I finish this somewhat didactic chat. You will admit that I have never
prosed so much before, but the period and the
subject seem to encourage it. I skip Sterne,
for I have no great sympathy with his finicky
methods. And I skip Miss Burney's novels,
as being feminine reflections of the great masters who had just preceded her. But Goldsmith's "Vicar of Wakefield" surely deserves

one paragraph to itself. There is a book
which is tinged throughout, as was all Goldsmith's work, with a beautiful nature. No
one who had not a fine heart could have written it, just as no one without a fine heart could
have written "The Deserted Village." How
strange it is to think of old Johnson patroniz-
ing or snubbing the shrinking Irishman, when
both in poetry, in fiction, and in the drama the
latter has proved himself far the greater man.
But here is an object-lesson of how the facts
of life may be treated without offense. Nothing is shirked. It is all faced and duly recorded. Yet if I wished to set before the sensitive mind of a young girl a book which would
prepare her for life without in any way con-
taminating her delicacy of feeling, there is
no book which I should choose so readily as
"The Vicar of Wakefield."

So much for the eighteenth-century novelists. They have a shelf of their own in the case,
and a corner of their own in my brain. For

years you may never think of them, and then
suddenly some stray word or train of thought
leads straight to them, and you look at them
and love them, and rejoice that you know
them.   But let us pass to something which
may interest you more.

If statistics could be taken in the various
free libraries of the kingdom to prove the comparative popularity of different novelists with
the public, I think that it is quite certain that
Mr. George Meredith would come out very
low indeed.   If, on the other hand, a number
of authors were convened to determine which
of their fellow-craftsmen they considered the
greatest and the most stimulating to their own
minds, I am equally confident that Mr. Meredith would have a vast preponderance of votes.
Indeed, his only conceivable rival would be
Mr. Hardy.   It becomes an interesting study,
therefore, why there should be such a diver-
gence of opinion as to his merits, and what the
qualities are which have repelled so many

readers, and yet have attracted those whose opinion must be allowed to have a special weight.

The most obvious reason is his complete unconventionality. The public read to be amused. The novelist reads to have new light thrown upon his art. To read Meredith is *not* a mere amusement; it is an intellectual exercise, a kind of mental dumb-bell with which you develop your thinking powers. Your mind is in a state of tension the whole time that you are reading him.

If you will follow my nose as the sportsman follows that of his pointer, you will observe that these remarks are excited by the presence of my beloved "Richard Feverel," which lurks in yonder corner. What a great book it is, how wise and how witty! Others of the master's novels may be more characteristic or more profound, but for my own part it is the one which I would always present to the new-comer who had not yet come under the influence. I think that I should put it third

after "Vanity Fair" and "The Cloister and
the Hearth" if I had to name the three novels
which I admire most in the Victorian era.
The book was published, I believe, in 1859,
and it is almost incredible, and says little for
the discrimination of critics or public, that it
was nearly twenty years before a second edition was needed.

But there are never effects without causes,
however inadequate the cause may be. What
was it that stood in the way of the book's success? Undoubtedly it was the style. And
yet it is subdued and tempered here with little
of the luxuriance and exuberance which it attained in the later works. But it was an inno-
vation, and it stalled off both the public and
the critics. They regarded it, no doubt, as an
affectation, as Carlyle's had been considered
twenty years before, forgetting that in the case
of an original genius style is an organic
thing, part of the man as much as the color
of his eyes. It is not, to quote Carlyle, a
shirt to be taken on and off at pleasure, but

a skin, eternally fixed. And this strange, powerful style, how is it to be described? Best, perhaps, in his own strong words, when he spoke of Carlyle with perhaps the *arrière pensée* that the words would apply as strongly to himself.

"His favorite author," says he, "was one writing on heroes in a style resembling either early architecture or utter dilapidation, so loose and rough it seemed. A wind-in-the-orchard style that tumbled down here and there an appreciable fruit with uncouth bluster, sentences without commencements running to abrupt endings and smoke, like waves against a sea-wall, learned dictionary words giving a hand to street slang, and accents falling on them haphazard, like slant rays from driving clouds; all the pages in a breeze, the whole book producing a kind of electrical agitation in the mind and joints."

What a wonderful description and example of style! And how vivid is the impression left by such expressions as "all the pages in a breeze." As a comment on Carlyle, and as a sample of Meredith, the passage is equally perfect.

Well, "Richard Feverel" has come into its own at last. I confess to having a strong belief in the critical discernment of the public. I do not think good work is often overlooked. Literature, like water, finds its true level. Opinion is slow to form, but it sets true at last. I am sure that if the critics were to unite to praise a bad book or to damn a good one they could (and continually do) have a five-year influence, but it would in no wise affect the final result. Sheridan said that if all the fleas in his bed had been unanimous, they could have pushed him out of it. I do not think that any unanimity of critics has ever pushed a good book out of literature.

Among the minor excellences of "Richard Feverel"—excuse the prolixity of an enthusiast—are the scattered aphorisms which are worthy of a place among our British proverbs. What could be more exquisite than this,

"Who rises from prayer a better man his prayer is answered"; or this, "Expediency is man's wisdom. Doing right is God's"; or, "All great thoughts come from the heart"? Good are the words "The coward amongst us is he who sneers at the failings of humanity," and a healthy optimism rings in the phrase "There is for the mind but one grasp of happiness; from that uppermost pinnacle of wisdom whence we see that this world is well designed." In more playful mood is "Woman is the last thing which will be civilized by man." Let us hurry away abruptly, for he who starts quotation from "Richard Feverel" is lost.

He has, as you see, a goodly line of his brothers beside him. There are the Italian ones, "Sandra Belloni," and "Vittoria"; there is "Rhoda Fleming," which carried Stevenson off his critical feet; "Beauchamp's Career," too, dealing with obsolete politics. No great writer should spend himself upon a temporary theme. It is like the beauty who is painted in some passing fashion of gown. She tends to become obsolete along with her frame. Here also is the dainty "Diana," the egoist with immortal Willoughby Pattern, eternal type of masculine selfishness, and "Harry Richmond," the first chapters of which are, in my opinion, among the finest pieces of narrative prose in the language. That great mind would have worked in any form which his age had favored. He is a novelist by accident. As an Elizabethan he would have been a great dramatist; under Queen Anne a great essayist. But whatever medium he worked in, he must equally have thrown the image of a great brain and a great soul.

VIII

WE have left our eighteenth-century novelists—Fielding, Richardson, and Smollett—safely behind us, with all their solidity and their audacity, their sincerity, and their coarseness of fiber. They have brought us, as you perceive, to the end of the shelf. What, not wearied? Ready for yet another? Let us run down this next row, then, and I will tell you a few things which may be of interest, though they will be dull enough if you have not been born with that love of books in your heart which is among the choicest gifts of the gods. If that is wanting, then one might as well play music to the deaf, or walk round the Academy with the color-blind, as appeal to the book-sense of an unfortunate who has it not.

There is this old brown volume in the cor-

ner. How it got there I cannot imagine,
for it is one of those which I bought for threepence out of the remnant box in Edinburgh,
and its weather-beaten comrades are up yonder in the back gallery, while this one has el-
bowed its way among the quality in the stalls.
But it is worth a word or two. Take it out
and handle it! See how swarthy it is, how
squat, with how bullet-proof a cover of scal-
ing leather. Now open the fly-leaf *"Ex
libris* Guilielmi Whyte. 1672" in faded yellow ink. I wonder who William Whyte may
have been, and what he did upon earth in the
reign of the merry monarch. A prag-
matical seventeenth-century lawyer, I should
judge, by that hard, angular writing. The
date of issue is 1642, so it was printed just
about the time when the Pilgrim Fathers
were settling down into their new American
home, and the first Charles's head was still
firm upon his shoulders, though a little puz-
zled, no doubt, at what was going around it.
The book is in Latin—though Cicero might

not have admitted it—and it treats of the laws of warfare.

I picture some pedantic Dugald Dalgetty bearing it about under his buff coat, or down in his holster, and turning up the reference for every fresh emergency which occurred. "Hullo! here's a well!" says he. "I wonder if I may poison it?" Out comes the book, and he runs a dirty forefinger down the index. *"Ob fas est aquam hostis venere,"* etc. "Tut, tut, it's not allowed. But here are some of the enemy in a barn? What about that?" *"Ob fas est hostem incendio,"* etc. "Yes; he says we may. Quick, Ambrose, up with the straw and the tinder box." Warfare was no child's play about the time when Tilly sacked Magdeburg, and Cromwell turned his hand from the mash tub to the sword. It might not be much better now in a long campaign, when men were hardened and embittered. Many of these laws are unrepealed, and it is less than a century since highly disciplined British troops claimed their dreadful rights at Badajos and Rodrigo. Recent European wars have been so short that discipline and humanity have not had time to go to pieces, but a long war would show that man is ever the same, and that civilization is the thinnest of veneers.

Now you see that whole row of books which takes you at one sweep nearly across the shelf? I am rather proud of those, for they are my collection of Napoleonic military memoirs. There is a story told of an illiterate millionaire who gave a wholesale dealer an order for a copy of all books in any language treating of any aspect of Napoleon's career. He thought it would fill a case in his library. He was somewhat taken aback, however, when in a few weeks he received a message from the dealer that he had got 40,000 volumes, and awaited instructions as to whether he should send them on as an instalment, or wait for a complete set. The figures may not be exact, but at least they bring home the impossibility of exhausting the subject, and the danger of losing one's self for years in a huge labyrinth of reading, which may end by leaving no very definite impression upon your mind. But one might, perhaps, take a corner of it, as I have done here in the military memoirs, and there one might hope to get some finality.

Here is Marbot at this end—the first of all soldier books in the world. This is the complete three-volume French edition, with red and gold cover, smart and *débonnaire* like its author. Here he is in one frontispiece with his pleasant, round, boyish face, as a Captain of his beloved Chasseurs. And here in the other is the grizzled old bull-dog as a full general, looking as full of fight as ever. It was a real blow to me when some one began to throw doubts upon the authenticity of Marbot's memoirs. Homer may be dissolved into a crowd of skin-clad bards. Even Shakespeare may be jostled in his throne of honor by plausible -Baconians; but the human, the gallant, the inimitable Marbot! His book is that which gives us the best picture by far of the Napoleonic soldiers, and to me they are even more interesting than their great leader, though his must ever be the most singular figure in history. But those soldiers, with their hugh shakoes, their hairy knapsacks, and their hearts of steel—what men they were! And what a latent power there must be in this French nation which could go on pouring out the blood of its sons for twenty-three years with hardly a pause!

It took all that time to work off the hot ferment which the Revolution had left in men's veins. And they were not exhausted, for the very last fight which the French fought was the finest of all. Proud as we are of our infantry at Waterloo, it was really with the French cavalry that the greenest laurels of that great epic rested. They got the better of our own cavalry, they took our guns again and again, they swept a large portion of our allies from the field, and finally they rode off unbroken, and as full of fight as ever. Read Gronow's "Memoirs," that chatty little yellow volume yonder which brings all that age back to us more vividly than any more pretentious work, and you will find the chivalrous admiration which our officers expressed at the fine performance of the French horsemen.

It must be admitted that, looking back upon history, we have not always been good allies, nor yet generous, co-partners in the battlefield. The first is the fault of our politics, where one party rejoices to break what the other has bound. The makers of the Treaty are staunch enough, as the Tories were under Pitt and Castlereagh, or the Whigs at the time of Queen Anne, but sooner or later the others must come in. At the end of the Marlborough wars we suddenly vamped up a peace and left our allies in the lurch, on account of a change in domestic politics. We did the same with Frederick the Great, and would have done it in the Napoleonic days if Fox could have controlled the country. And as to our partners of the battlefield, how little

we have ever said that is hearty as to the
splendid staunchness of the Prussians at
Waterloo. You have to read the Frenchman,
Houssaye, to get a central view and to understand the part they played. Think of old
Blucher, seventy years old, and ridden over by
a regiment of charging cavalry the day before, yet swearing that he would come to Wellington if he had to be strapped to his horse.
He nobly redeemed his promise.

The loss of the Prussians at Waterloo was
not far short of our own. You would not
know it, to read our historians. And then the
abuse of our Belgian allies has been overdone.
Some of them fought splendidly, and one
brigade of infantry had a share in the critical
instant when the battle was turned. This
also you would not learn from British sources.
Look at our Portuguese allies also! They
trained into magnificent troops, and one of
Wellington's earnest desires was to have ten
thousand of them for his Waterloo campaign.
It was a Portuguese who first topped the ram-

part of Badajos. They have never had their
due credit, nor have the Spaniards either, for,
though often defeated, it was their uncon-
querable pertinacity which played a great
part in the struggle. No; I do not think that
we are very amiable partners, but I suppose
that all national history may be open to a similar charge.

It must be confessed that Marbot's details
are occasionally a little hard to believe. Never
in the pages of Lever has there been such a
series of hairbreadth escapes and dare-devil
exploits. Surely he stretched it a little sometimes. You may remember his adventure at
Eylau—I think it was Eylau—how a cannon-
ball, striking the top of his helmet, paralyzed
him by the concussion of his spine; and how,
on a Russian officer running forward to cut
him down, his horse bit the man's face nearly
off. This was the famous charger which sav-
aged everything until Marbot, having bought
it for next to nothing, cured it by thrusting
a boiling leg of mutton into its mouth when

it tried to bite him. It certainly does need
a robust faith to get over these incidents.
And yet, when one reflects upon the hundreds
of battles and skirmishes which a Napoleonic
officer must have endured—how they must
have been the uninterrupted routine of his
life from the first dark hair upon his lip to the
first gray one upon his head, it is presumptu-
ous to say what may or may not have been
possible in such unparalleled careers. At any
rate, be it fact or fiction—fact it is, in my
opinion, with some artistic touching up of the
high lights—there are few books which I
could not spare from my shelves better than
the memoirs of the gallant Marbot.

I dwell upon this particular book because
it is the best; but take the whole line, and
there is not one which is not full of interest.
Marbot gives you the point of view of the
officer. So does De Ségfur and De Fezensac
and Colonel Gonville, each in some different
branch of the service. But some are from the
pens of the men in the ranks, and they are

even more graphic than the others. Here, for example, are the papers of good old Cogniet, who was a grenadier of the Guard, and could neither read nor write until after the great wars were over. A tougher soldier never went into battle. Here is Sergeant Bourgogne, also with his dreadful account of that nightmare campaign in Russia, and the gallant Chevillet, trumpeter of Chasseurs, with his matter-of-fact account of all that he saw, where the daily "combat" is sandwiched in betwixt the real business of the day, which was foraging for his frugal breakfast and supper. There is no better writing, and no easier reading, than the records of these men of action.

A Briton cannot help asking himself, as he realizes what men these were, what would have happened if 150,000 Cogniets and Bourgognes, with Marbots to lead them, and the great captain of all time in the prime of his vigor at their head, had made their landing in Kent? For months it was touch-and-go. A single naval slip which left the Channel clear would have been followed by an embarkation from Boulogne, which had been brought by constant practice to so incredibly fine a point that the last horse was aboard within two hours of the start. Any evening might have seen the whole host upon the Pevensey Flats. What then? We know what Humbert did with a handful of men in Ireland, and the story is not reassuring. Conquest, of course, is unthinkable. The world in arms could not do that. But Napoleon never thought of the conquest of Britain. He has expressly disclaimed it. What he did contemplate was a gigantic raid in which he would do so much damage that for years to come England would be occupied at home in picking up the pieces, instead of having energy to spend abroad in thwarting his Continental plans.

Portsmouth, Plymouth, and Sheerness in flames, with London either leveled to the ground, or ransomed at his own figure—that was a more feasible programme. Then, with

the united fleets of conquered Europe at
his back, enormous armies and an inexhausti-
ble treasury, swollen with the ransom of Britain, he could turn to that conquest of America which would win back the old colonies of
France and leave him master of the world.
If the worst happened and he had met his
Waterloo upon the South Downs, he would
have done again what he did in Egypt and
once more in Russia: hurried back to France
in a swift vessel, and still have force enough
to hold his own upon the Continent. It
would, no doubt, have been a big stake to lay
upon the table—150,000 of his best—but he
could play again if he lost; while, if he won,
he cleared the board. A fine game—if little
Nelson had not stopped it, and with one blow
fixed the edge of salt water as the limit of
Napoleon's power.

There's the cast of a medal on the top of
that cabinet which will bring it all close home
to you. It is taken from the die of the medal
which Napoleon had arranged to issue on the

day that he reached London. It serves, at any rate, to show that his great muster was not a bluff, but that he really did mean serious business. On one side is his head. On the other France is engaged in strangling and throwing to earth a curious fish-tailed creature, which stands for perfidious Albion. "Frappé à Londres" is printed on one part of it, and "La Descente dans Angleterre" upon another. Struck to commemorate a conquest, it remains now as a souvenir of a fiasco. But it was a close call.

By the way, talking of Napoleon's flight from Egypt, did you ever see a curious little book called, if I remember right, "Intercepted Letters?" No; I have no copy upon this shelf, but a friend is more fortunate. It shows the almost incredible hatred which existed at the end of the eighteenth century between the two nations, descending even to the most petty personal annoyance. On this occasion the British Government intercepted a mail-bag of letters coming from French officers in Egypt to their friends at home, and they either published them, or at least allowed them to be published, in the hope, no doubt, of causing domestic complications. Was ever a more despicable action? But who knows what other injuries had been inflicted to draw forth such a retaliation? I have myself seen a burned and mutilated British mail lying where De Wet had left it; but suppose the refinement of his vengeance had gone so far as to publish it, what a thunder-bolt it might have been!

As to the French officers, I have read their letters, though even after a century one had a feeling of guilt when one did so. But, on the whole, they are a credit to the writers, and give the impression of a noble and chivalrous set of men. Whether they were all addressed to the right people is another matter, and therein lay the poisoned sting of this most un-British affair. As to the monstrous things which were done upon the other side, remember the arrest of all the poor British tourists and commercials who chanced to be in France when the war was renewed in 1803. They had run over in all trust and confidence for a little outing and change of air. They certainly got it, for Napoleon's steel grip fell upon them and they rejoined their families in 1814. He must have had a heart of adamant and a will of iron. Look at his conduct over the naval prisoners. The natural proceeding would have been to exchange them. For some reason he did not think it good policy to do so. All representations from the British Government were set aside, save in the case of the higher officers. Hence the miseries of the hulks and the dreadful prison barracks in England. Hence also the unhappy idlers of Verdun. What splendid loyalty there must have been in those humble Frenchmen which never allowed them for one instant to turn bitterly upon the author of all their great misfortunes. It is all brought vividly home by the description of their prisons given by Borrow in "Lavengro." This is the passage—

"What a strange appearance had those mighty casernes, with their blank, blind walls, without windows or grating, and their slanting roofs, out of which, through orifices where the tiles had been removed, would be protruded dozens of grim heads, feasting their prison-sick eyes on the wide expanse of country unfolded from their airy height. Ah! there was much misery in those casernes; and from those roofs, doubtless, many a wistful look was turned in the direction of lovely France. Much had the poor inmates to endure, and much to complain of, to the disgrace of England be it said—of England, in general so kind and bountiful. Rations of carrion meat, and bread from which I have seen the very hounds occasionally turn away, were unworthy entertainment even for the most ruffian enemy, when helpless and captive; and such, alas! was the fare in those casernes. And then, those visits, or rather ruthless inroads, called in the slang of the place 'straw-plait hunts,' when in pursuit of a contraband article,

which the prisoners, in order to procure themselves a few of the necessaries and comforts
of existence, were in the habit of making, red-
coated battalions were marched into the
prisons, who, with the bayonet's point, carried
havoc and ruin into every poor convenience
which ingenious wretchedness had been endea-
voring to raise around it; and then the tri-
umphant exit with the miserable booty, and
worst of all, the accursed bonfire, on the bar-
rack parade of the plait contraband, beneath
the view of glaring eyeballs from those lofty
roofs, amid the hurrahs of the troops frequently drowned in the curses poured down
from above like a tempest-shower, or in the
terrific war-whoop of 'Vive l'Empereur!'"

There is a little vignette of Napoleon's men
in captivity. Here is another which is worth
preserving of the bearing of his veterans when
wounded on the field of battle. It is from
Mercer's recollections of the Battle of Waterloo. Mercer had spent the day firing case into

the French cavalry at ranges from fifty to two
hundred yards, losing two-thirds of his own
battery in the process. In the evening he
had a look at some of his own grim handi-
work.

"I had satisfied my curiosity at Hougou-
mont, and was retracing my steps up the hill
when my attention was called to a group of
wounded Frenchmen by the calm, dignified,
and soldier-like oration addressed by one of
them to the rest. I cannot, like Livy, com-
pose a fine harangue for my hero, and, of
course, I could not retain the precise words,
but the import of them was to exhort them
to bear their sufferings with fortitude; not to
repine, like women or children, at what every
soldier should have made up his mind to suffer
as the fortune of war, but above all, to remember that they were surrounded by Englishmen,
before whom they ought to be doubly careful
not to disgrace themselves by displaying such
an unsoldier-like want of fortitude.

"The speaker was sitting on the ground with his lance stuck upright beside him—an old veteran with thick bushy, grizzly beard, countenance like a lion—a lancer of the old guard, and no doubt had fought in many a field. One hand was flourished in the air as he spoke, the other, severed at the wrist, lay on the earth beside him; one ball (case-shot, probably) had entered his body, another had broken his leg. His suffering, after a night of exposure so mangled, must have been great; yet he betrayed it not. His bearing was that of a Roman, or perhaps an Indian warrior, and I could fancy him concluding appropriately his speech in the words of the Mexican king, 'And I too; am I on a bed of roses?' "

What a load of moral responsibility upon one man! But his mind was insensible to moral responsibility. Surely if it had not been it must have been crushed beneath it. Now, if you want to understand the character of Napoleon—but surely I must take a fresh start before I launch on so portentous a subject as that.

But before I leave the military men let me, for the credit of my own country, after that infamous incident of the letters, indicate these six well-thumbed volumes of "Napier's History." This is the story of the great Peninsular War, by one who fought through it himself, and in no history has a more chivalrous and manly account been given of one's enemy. Indeed, Napier seems to me to push it too far, for his admiration appears to extend not only to the gallant soldiers who opposed him, but to the character and to the ultimate aims of their leader. He was, in fact, a political follower of Charles James Fox, and his heart seems to have been with the enemy even at the moment when he led his men most desperately against them. In the verdict of history the action of those men who, in their honest zeal for freedom, inflamed somewhat by political strife, turned against their own country, when it was in truth the Champion of Freedom, and ap-

proved of a military despot of the most un-
compromising kind, seems wildly foolish.

But if Napier's politics may seem strange,
his soldiering was splendid, and his prose
among the very best that I know.   There are
passages in that work—the one which describes
the breach of Badajos, that of the charge of
the Fusiliers at Albuera, and that of the
French advance at Fuentes d'Onoro—which
once read haunt the mind for ever.   The book
is a worthy monument of a great national epic.
Alas! for the pregnant sentence with which it
closes, "So ended the great war, and with it
all memory of the services of the veterans."
Was there ever a British war of which the
same might not have been written?

The quotation which I have given from
Mercer's book turns my thoughts in the direction of the British military reminiscences of
that period, less numerous, less varied, and less
central than the French, but full of character
and interest all the same.   I have found that
if I am turned loose in a large library, after

hesitating over covers for half an hour or so, it is usually a book of soldier memoirs which I take down. Man is never so interesting as when he is thoroughly in earnest, and no one is so earnest as he whose life is at stake upon the event. But of all types of soldier the best is the man who is keen upon his work, and yet has general culture which enables him to see that work in its due perspective, and to sympathize with the gentler aspirations of mankind. Such a man is Mercer, an ice-cool fighter, with a sense of discipline and decorum which prevented him from moving when a bombshell was fizzing between his feet, and yet a man of thoughtful and philosophic temperament, with a weakness for solitary musings, for children, and for flowers. He has written for all time the classic account of a great battle, seen from the point of view of a battery commander. Many others of Wellington's soldiers wrote their personal reminiscences. You can get them, as I have them there, in the pleasant abridgment of "Wellington's Men" (admi-

rably edited by Dr. Fitchett)—Anton the
Highlander, Harris the rifleman, and Kincaid
of the same corps. It is a most singular fate
which has made an Australian nonconformist
clergyman the most sympathetic and eloquent
reconstructor of those old heroes, but it is a
noble example of that unity of the British race,
which in fifty scattered lands still mourns or
rejoices over the same historic record.

And just one word, before I close down this
over-long and too discursive chatter, on the
subject of yonder twin red volumes which
flank the shelf. They are Maxwell's "History
of Wellington," and I do not think you will
find a better or more readable one. The
reader must ever feel towards the great soldier what his own immediate followers felt,
respect rather than affection. One's failure to
attain a more affectionate emotion is alleviated
by the knowledge that it was the last thing
which he invited or desired. "Don't be a
damned fool, sir!" was his exhortation to the
good citizen who had paid him a compliment.

It was a curious, callous nature, brusque and limited. The hardest huntsman learns to love his hounds, but he showed no affection and a good deal of contempt for the men who had been his instruments. "They are the scum of the earth," said he. "All English soldiers are fellows who have enlisted for drink. That is the plain fact—they have all enlisted for drink." His general orders were full of un-deserved reproaches at a time when the most lavish praise could hardly have met the real deserts of his army. When the wars were done he saw little, save in his official capacity, of his old comrades-in-arms. And yet, from major-general to drummer-boy, he was the man whom they would all have elected to serve under, had the work to be done once more. As one of them said, "The sight of his long nose was worth ten thousand men on a field of bat-tle." They were themselves a leathery breed, and cared little for the gentler amenities so long as the French were well drubbed.

His mind, which was comprehensive and

alert in warfare, was singularly limited in civil affairs. As a statesman he was so constant an example of devotion to duty, self-sacrifice, and high disinterested character, that the country was the better for his presence. But he fiercely opposed Catholic Emancipation, the Reform Bill, and everything upon which our modern life is founded. He could never be brought to see that a pyramid should stand on its base and not on its apex, and that the larger the pyramid, the broader should be the base. Even in military affairs he was averse from every change, and I know of no improvements which came from his initiative during all those years when his authority was supreme. The floggings which broke a man's spirit and self-respect, the leathern stock which hampered his movements, all the old traditional *régime* found a champion in him. On the other hand, he strongly opposed the introduction of the percussion cap as opposed to the flint and steel in the musket. Neither in war nor in politics did he rightly judge the future.

And yet in reading his letters and dispatches, one is surprised sometimes at the incisive thought and its vigorous expression. There is a passage in which he describes the way in which his soldiers would occasionally desert into some town which he was besieging. "They knew," he writes, "that they must be taken, for when we lay our bloody hands upon a place we are sure to take it, sooner or later; but they liked being dry and under cover, and then that extraordinary caprice which always pervades the English character! Our deserters are very badly treated by the enemy; those who deserted in France were treated as the lowest of mortals, slaves and scavengers. Nothing but English caprice can account for it; just what makes our noblemen associate with stage-coach drivers, and become stage-coach drivers themselves." After reading that passage, how often does the phrase "the extraordinary caprice which always pervades the English character" come back as one observes some fresh manifestation of it!

But let not my last note upon the great duke be a carping one.   Rather let my final sentence be one which will remind you of his frugal and abstemious life, his carpetless floor and little camp bed, his precise courtesy which left no humblest letter unanswered, his courage which never flinched, his tenacity which never faltered, his sense of duty which made his life one long unselfish effort on behalf of what seemed to him to be the highest interest of the State.   Go down and stand by the huge granite sarcophagus in the dim light of the crypt of St. Paul's, and in the hush of that austere spot, cast back your mind to the days when little England alone **stood** firm against the greatest soldier and the greatest army that the world has ever known.   Then you feel what this dead man stood for, and you pray that we may still find such another amongst us when the clouds gather once again.

You see that the literature of Waterloo is well represented in my small military library. Of all books dealing with the personal view of

the matter, I think that "Siborne's Letters,"
which is a collection of the narratives of sur-
viving officers made by Siborne in the year
1827, is the most interesting. Gronow's account is also very vivid and interesting. Of
the strategical narratives, Houssaye's book is
my favorite. Taken from the French point
of view, it gets the actions of the allies in truer
perspective than any English or German account can do; but there is a fascination about
that great combat which makes every narrative that bears upon it of enthralling interest.

Wellington used to say that too much was
made of it, and that one would imagine that
the British Army had never fought a battle
before. It was a characteristic speech, but it
must be admitted that the British Army never
had, as a matter of fact, for many centuries
fought a battle which was finally decisive of
a great European war. There lies the peren-
nial interest of the incident, that it was the last
act of that long-drawn drama, and that to the
very fall of the curtain no man could tell how

the play would end—"the nearest run thing
that ever you saw"—that was the victor's description. It is a singular thing that during
those twenty-five years of incessant fighting
the material and methods of warfare made so
little progress. So far as I know, there was
no great change in either between 1789 and
1815. The breech-loader, heavy artillery, the
ironclad, all great advances in the art of war,
have been invented in time of peace. There
are some improvements so obvious, and at the
same time so valuable, that it is extraordinary
that they were not adopted. Signaling, for
example, whether by heliograph or by flag-
waving, would have made an immense difference in the Napoleonic campaigns. The principle of the semaphore was well known, and
Belgium, with its numerous windmills, would
seem to be furnished with natural semaphores.
Yet in the four days during which the campaign of Waterloo was fought, the whole
scheme of military operations on both sides
was again and again imperilled, and finally

in the case of the French brought to utter ruin
by lack of that intelligence which could so
easily have been conveyed. June 18th was at
intervals a sunshiny day—a four-inch glass
mirror would have put Napoleon in communi-
cation with Gruchy, and the whole history of
Europe might have been altered. Wellington
himself suffered dreadfully from defective information which might have been easily supplied. The unexpected presence of the
French army was first discovered at four in
the morning of June 15. It was of enormous
importance to get the news rapidly to Wellington at Brussels that he might instantly con-
centrate his scattered forces on the best line of
resistance—yet, through the folly of sending
only a single messenger, this vital information did not reach him until three in the after-
noon, the distance being thirty miles. Again,
when Blucher was defeated at Ligny on the
16th, it was of enormous importance that Wellington should know at once the line of his retreat so as to prevent the French from driving

a wedge between them.   The single Prussian officer who was despatched with this information was wounded, and never reached his destination, and it was only next day that Wellington learned the Prussian plans.   On what tiny things does History depend!

IX

THE contemplation of my fine little regiment of French military memoirs had brought me to the question of Napoleon himself, and you see that I have a very fair line dealing with him also. There is Scott's life, which is not entirely a success. His ink was too precious to be shed in such a venture. But here are the three volumes of the physician Bourrienne—that Bourrienne who knew him so well. Does any one ever know a man so well as his doctor? They are quite excellent and admirably translated. Meneval also—the patient Meneval—who wrote for untold hours to dictation at ordinary talking speed, and yet was expected to be legible and to make no mistakes. At least his master could not fairly criticise his legibility, for is it not on record that when Napoleon's holograph account of an engagement was laid before the President of the Senate, the worthy man thought that it was a drawn plan of the battle? Meneval survived his master and has left an excellent and intimate account of him. There is Constant's account, also written from that point of view in which it is proverbial that no man is a hero. But of all the vivid terrible pictures of Napoleon the most haunting is by a man who never saw him and whose book was not directly dealing with him. I mean Taine's account of him, in the first volume of "Les Origines de la France Contemporaine." You can never forget it when once you have read it. He produces his effect in a wonderful, and to me a novel, way. He does not, for example, say in mere crude words that Napoleon had a more than mediæval Italian cunning. He presents a succession of documents—gives a series of contemporary instances to prove it. Then, having got that fixed in your head by blow after blow, he passes on to another phase of his character, his cold-hearted amorousness, his power of work, his spoiled child wilfulness, or some other quality, and piles up his illustrations of that.   Instead, for example, of saying that the Emperor had a marvelous memory for detail, we have the account of the head of Artillery laying the list of all the guns in France before his master, who looked over it and remarked, "Yes, but you have omitted two in a fort near Dieppe." So the man is gradually etched in with indelible ink.   It is a wonderful figure of which you are conscious in the end, the figure of an archangel, but surely of an archangel of darkness.

We will, after Taine's method, take one fact and let it speak for itself.   Napoleon left a legacy in a codicil to his will to a man who tried to assassinate Wellington.   There is the mediæval Italian again!   He was no more a Corsican than the Englishman born in India is a Hindoo.   Read the lives of the Borgias, the Sforzas, the Medicis, and of all the lustful, cruel, broad-minded, art-loving, talented despots of the little Italian States, including

Genoa, from which the Buonapartes migrated. There at once you get the real descent of the man, with all the stigmata clear upon him— the outward calm, the inward passion, the layer of snow above the volcano, everything which characterized the old despots of his native land, the pupils of Machiavelli, but all raised to the dimensions of genius. You can whitewash him as you may, but you will never get a layer thick enough to cover the stain of that cold-blooded deliberate endorsement of his noble adversary's assassination.

Another book which gives an extraordinarily vivid picture of the man is this one—the Memoirs of Madame de Remusat. She was in daily contact with him at the Court, and she studied him with those quick critical eyes of a clever woman, the most unerring things in life when they are not blinded by love. If you have read those pages, you feel that you know him as if you had yourself seen and talked with him. His singular mixture of the small and the great, his huge sweep of imagination, his very limited knowledge, his intense egotism, his impatience of obstacles, his boorishness, his gross impertinence to women, his diabolical playing upon the weak side of every one with whom he came in contact—they make up among them one of the most striking of historical portraits.

Most of my books deal with the days of his greatness, but here, you see, is a three-volume account of those weary years at St. Helena. Who can help pitying the mewed eagle? And yet if you play the great game you must pay a stake. This was the same man who had a royal duke shot in a ditch because he was a danger to his throne. Was not he himself a danger to every throne in Europe? Why so harsh a retreat as St. Helena, you say? Remember that he had been put in a milder one before, that he had broken away from it, and that the lives of fifty thousand men had paid for the mistaken leniency. All this is forgotten now, and the pathetic picture of the modern Prometheus chained to his rock and devoured by the vultures of his own bitter thoughts, is the one impression which the world has retained. It is always so much easier to follow the emotions than the reason, especially where a cheap magnanimity and second-hand generosity are involved. But reason must still insist that Europe's treatment of Napoleon was not vindictive, and that Hudson Lowe was a man who tried to live up to the trust which had been committed to him by his country.

It was certainly not a post from which any one would hope for credit. If he were slack and easy-going all would be well. But there would be the chance of a second flight with its consequences. If he were strict and assiduous he would be assuredly represented as a petty tyrant. "I am glad when you are on outpost," said Lowe's general in some campaign, "for then I am sure of a sound rest." He was on outpost at St. Helena, and because he was true to his duties Europe (France included) had a sound rest. But he purchased it at the price of his own reputation. The

greatest schemer in the world, having nothing
else on which to vent his energies, turned them
all to the task of vilifying his guardian. It
was natural enough that he who had never
known control should not brook it now. It is
natural also that sentimentalists who have not
thought of the details should take the Emper-
or's point of view. What is deplorable, however, is that our own people should be misled
by one-sided accounts, and that they should
throw to the wolves a man who was serving his
country in a post of anxiety and danger, with
such responsibility upon him as few could ever
have endured. Let them remember Montho-
lon's remark: "An angel from heaven would
not have satisfied us." Let them recall also
that Lowe with ample material never once
troubled to state his own case. *"Je fais mon
devoir et suis indifférent pour le reste,"* said
he, in his interview with the Emperor. They
were no idle words.

Apart from this particular epoch, French
literature, which is so rich in all its branches,

is richest of all in its memoirs. Whenever there was anything of interest going forward there was always some kindly gossip who knew all about it, and was ready to set it down for the benefit of posterity. Our own history has not nearly enough of these charming side-lights. Look at our sailors in the Napoleonic wars, for example. They played an epoch-making part. For nearly twenty years Freedom was a Refugee upon the seas. Had our navy been swept away, then all Europe would have been one organized despotism. At times everybody was against us, fighting against their own direct interests under the pressure of that terrible hand. We fought on the waters with the French, with the Spaniards, with the Danes, with the Russians, with the Turks, even with our American kinsmen. Middies grew into post-captains, and admirals into dotards during that prolonged struggle. And what have we in literature to show for it all? Marryat's novels, many of which are founded upon personal experience, Nelson's and Collingwood's letters, Lord Cochrane's biography—that is about all. I wish we had more of Collingwood, for he wielded a fine pen. Do you remember the sonorous opening of his Trafalgar message to his captains?—

"The ever to be lamented death of Lord Viscount Nelson, Duke of Bronte, the Commander-in-Chief, who fell in the action of the 21st, in the arms of Victory, covered with glory, whose memory will be ever dear to the British Navy and the British Nation; whose zeal for the honor of his king and for the interests of his country will be ever held up as a shining example for a British seaman—leaves to me a duty to return thanks, etc., etc."

It was a worthy sentence to carry such a message, written too in a raging tempest, with sinking vessels all around him. But in the main it is a poor crop from such a soil. No doubt our sailors were too busy to do much writing, but none the less one wonders that

among so many thousands there were not some
to understand what a treasure their experiences
would be to their descendants.   I can call to
mind the old three-deckers which used to rot in
Portsmouth Harbor, and I have often thought,
could they tell their tales, what a missing chapter in our literature they could supply.

It is not only in Napoleonic memoirs that
the French are so fortunate.   The almost
equally interesting age of Louis XIV. produced an even more wonderful series.   If you
go deeply into the subject you are amazed by
their number, and you feel as if every one at
the Court of the Roi Soleil had done what he
(or she) could to give away their neighbors.
Just to take the more obvious, there are St.
Simon's Memoirs—those in themselves give us
a more comprehensive and intimate view of the
age than anything I know of which treats of
the times of Queen Victoria.   Then there is
St. Evremond, who is nearly as complete.   Do
you want the view of a woman of quality?
There are the letters of Madame de Sévigné

(eight volumes of them), perhaps the most wonderful series of letters that any woman has ever penned. Do you want the confessions of a rake of the period? Here are the too salacious memoirs of the mischievous Duc de Roquelaure, not reading for the nursery certainly, not even for the boudoir, but a strange and **very intimate** picture of the times. All these books fit into each other, for the characters of the one reappear in the others. You come to know them quite familiarly before you have finished, their loves and their hates, their duels, their intrigues, and their ultimate fortunes. If you do not care to go so deeply into it you have only to put Julia Pardoe's four-volumed "Court of Louis XIV." upon your shelf, and you will find a very admirable condensation—or a distillation rather, for most of the salt is left behind. There is another book too—that big one on the bottom shelf—which holds it all between its brown and gold covers. An extravagance that—for it cost me some sovereigns—but it is something to have the portraits of all that wonderful galaxy, of Louis, of the devout Maintenon, of the frail Montespan, of Bossuet, Fénelon, Molière, Racine, Pascal, Condé, Turenne, and all the saints and sinners of the age. If you want to make yourself a present, and chance upon a copy of "The Court and Times of Louis XIV.," you will never think that your money has been wasted.

Well, I have bored you unduly, my patient friend, with my love of memoirs, Napoleonic and otherwise, which give a touch of human interest to the arid records of history. Not that history should be arid. It ought to be the most interesting subject upon earth, the story of ourselves, of our forefathers, of the human race, the events which made us what we are, and wherein, if Weismann's views hold the field, some microscopic fraction of this very body which for the instant we chance to inhabit may have borne a part. But unfortunately the power of accumulating knowledge and that of imparting it are two very different things, and the uninspired historian becomes merely the dignified compiler of an enlarged almanac. Worst of all, when a man does come along with fancy and imagination, who can breathe the breath of life into the dry bones, it is the fashion for the dryasdusts to belabor him as one who has wandered away from the orthodox path and must necessarily be inaccurate. So Froude was attacked. So also Macaulay in his day. But both will be read when the pedants are forgotten. If I were asked my very ideal of how history should be written, I think I should point to those two rows on yonder shelf, the one McCarthy's "History of Our Own Times," the other Lecky's "History of England in the Eighteenth Century." Curious that each should have been written by an Irishman, and that though of opposite politics and living in an age when Irish affairs have caused such bitterness, both should be conspicuous not merely for all literary graces, but for that broad toleration which sees every side of a question, and handles every problem from the point of view of the philosophic observer and never of the sectarian partisan.

By the way, talking of history, have you read Parkman's works? He was, I think, among the very greatest of the historians, and yet one seldom hears his name. A New England man by birth, and writing principally of the early history of the American Settlements and of French Canada, it is perhaps excusable that he should have no great vogue in England, but even among Americans I have found many who have not read him. There are four of his volumes in green and gold down yonder. "The Jesuits in Canada," and "Frontenac," but there are others, all of them well worth reading, "Pioneers of France," "Montcalm and Wolfe," "Discovery of the Great West," etc. Some day I hope to have a complete set.

Taking only that one book, "The Jesuits in Canada," it is worth a reputation in itself. And how noble a tribute is this which a man of Puritan blood pays to that wonderful Order!

He shows how in the heyday of their enthusiasm these brave soldiers of the Cross invaded
Canada as they did China and every other place
where danger was to be faced, and a horrible
death to be found. I don't care what faith a
man may profess, or whether he be a Christian at all, but he cannot read these true records without feeling that the very highest that
man has ever evolved in sanctity and devotion
was to be found among these marvelous men.
They were indeed the pioneers of civilization,
for apart from doctrines they brought among
the savages the highest European culture, and
in their own deportment an object-lesson of
how chastely, austerely, and nobly men could
live. France has sent myriads of brave men
on to her battlefields, but in all her long record
of glory I do not think that she can point to
any courage so steadfast and so absolutely
heroic as that of the men of the Iroquois Mission.

How nobly they lived makes the body of the
book, how serenely they died forms the end to

it. It is a tale which cannot even now be read without a shudder—a nightmare of horrors. Fanaticism may brace a man to hurl himself into oblivion, as the Mahdi's hordes did before Khartoum, but one feels that it is at least a higher development of such emotion, where men slowly and in cold blood endure so thankless a life, and welcome so dreadful an end. Every faith can equally boast its martyrs—a painful thought, since it shows how many thousands must have given their blood for error— but in testifying to their faith these brave men have testified to something more important still, to the subjugation of the body and to the absolute supremacy of the dominating spirit.

The story of Father Jogue is but one of many, and yet it is worth recounting, as showing the spirit of the men. He also was on the Iroquois Mission, and was so tortured and mutilated by his sweet parishioners that the very dogs used to howl at his distorted figure. He made his way back to France, not for any reason of personal rest or recuperation, but because he needed a special dispensation to say Mass. The Catholic Church has a regulation that a priest shall not be deformed, so that the savages with their knives had wrought better than they knew. He received his dispensation and was sent for by Louis XIV., who asked him what he could do for him. No doubt the assembled courtiers expected to hear him ask for the next vacant Bishopric. What he did actually ask for, as the highest favor, was to be sent back to the Iroquois Mission, where the savages signalized his arrival by burning him alive.

Parkman is worth reading, if it were only for his account of the Indians. Perhaps the very strangest thing about them, and the most unaccountable, is their small numbers. The Iroquois were one of the most formidable of tribes. They were of the Five Nations, whose scalping-parties wandered over an expanse of thousands of square miles. Yet there is good reason to doubt whether the whole five nations could have put as many thousand warriors in the field. It was the same with all the other tribes of North Americans, both in the east, the north, and the west. Their numbers were always insignificant. And yet they had that huge country to themselves, the best of climates, and plenty of food. Why was it that they did not people it thickly? It may be taken as a striking example of the purpose and design which run through the affairs of men, that at the very moment when the old world was ready to overflow the new world was empty to receive it. Had North America been peopled as China is peopled, the Europeans might have founded some settlements, but could never have taken possession of the Continent. Buffon has made the striking remark that the creative power appeared to have never had great vigor in America. He alluded to the abundance of the flora and fauna as compared with that of other great divisions of the earth's surface. Whether the numbers of the Indians are an illustration of the same fact, or whether there is some special cause, is beyond my very modest scientific attainments. When one reflects upon the countless herds of bison which used to cover the Western plains, or marks in the present day the race statistics of the French Canadians at one end of the Continent, and of the Southern negro at the other, it seems absurd to suppose that there is any geographical reason against Nature being as prolific here as elsewhere. However, these be deeper waters, and with your leave we will get back into my usual six-inch wading-depth once more.

X

I don't know how those two little books got in there. They are Henley's "Song of the Sword" and "Book of Verses." They ought to be over yonder in the rather limited Poetry Section. Perhaps it is that I like his work so, whether it be prose or verse, and so have put them ready to my hand. He was a remarkable man, a man who was very much greater than his work, great as some of his work was. I have seldom known a personality more magnetic and stimulating. You left his presence, as a battery leaves a generating station, charged up and full. He made you feel what a lot of work there was to be done, and how glorious it was to be able to do it, and how needful to get started upon it that very hour. With the frame and the vitality of a giant he was cruelly bereft of all outlet for his strength,

and so distilled it off in hot words, in warm
sympathy, in strong prejudices, in all manner
of human and stimulating emotions. Much
of the time and energy which might have built
an imperishable name for himself was spent in
encouraging others; but it was not waste, for
he left his broad thumb-mark upon all that
passed beneath it. A dozen second-hand Hen-
leys are fortifying our literature to-day.

Alas that we have so little of his very best!
for that very best was the finest of our time.
Few poets ever wrote sixteen consecutive lines
more noble and more strong than those which
begin with the well-known quatrain—

> " Out of the night that covers me,
>   Black as the pit from Pole to Pole,
> I thank whatever Gods there be
>   For my unconquerable soul."

It is grand literature, and it is grand pluck
too; for it came from a man who, through no
fault of his own, had been pruned, and pruned
again, like an ill-grown shrub, by the surgeon's
knife. When he said—

" In the fell clutch of Circumstance,
I have not winced nor cried aloud,
Beneath the bludgeonings of Chance
My head is bloody but unbowed."

It was not what Lady Byron called "The mimic woe" of the poet, but it was rather the grand defiance of the Indian warrior at the stake, whose proud soul can hold in hand his quivering body.

There were two quite distinct veins of poetry in Henley, each the very extreme from the other. The one was heroic, gigantic, running to large sweeping images and thundering words. Such are the "Song of the Sword" and much more that he has written, like the wild singing of some Northern scald. The other, and to my mind both the more characteristic and the finer side of his work, is delicate, precise, finely etched, with extraordinarily vivid little pictures drawn in carefully phrased and balanced English. Such are the "Hospital Verses," while the "London Voluntaries" stand midway between the two styles. What! you have not read the "Hospital Verses!"

Then get the "Book of Verses" and read them without delay. You will surely find something there which, for good or ill, is unique. You can name—or at least I can name—nothing to compare it with. Goldsmith and Crabbe have written of indoor themes; but their monotonous, if majestic meter, wearies the modern reader. But this is so varied, so flexible, so dramatic. It stands by itself. Confound the weekly journals and all the other lightning conductors which caused such a man to pass away, and to leave a total output of about five booklets behind him!

However, all this is an absolute digression, for the books had no business in this shelf at all. This corner is meant for chronicles of various sorts. Here are three in a line, which carry you over a splendid stretch of French (which usually means European) history, each, as luck would have it, beginning just about the time when the other leaves off. The first is Froissart, the second de Monstrelet, and the third de Comines. When you have read the

three you have the best contemporary account
first hand of considerably more than a century
—a fair slice out of the total written record of
the human race.

Froissart is always splendid.   If you desire
to avoid the mediæval French, which only a
specialist can read with pleasure, you can get
Lord Berners' almost equally mediæval, but
very charming English, or you can turn to a
modern translation, such as this one of Johnes.
A single page of Lord Berners is delightful;
but it is a strain, I think, to read bulky volumes in an archaic style.   Personally, I prefer
the modern, and even with that you have shown
some patience before you have reached the end
of that big second tome.

I wonder whether, at the time, the old
Hainault Canon had any idea of what he was
doing—whether it ever flashed across his mind
that the day might come when his book would
be the one great authority, not only about the
times in which he lived, but about the whole in-
stitution of chivalry?   I fear that it is far

more likely that his whole object was to gain some mundane advantage from the various barons and knights whose names and deeds he recounts. He has left it on record, for example, that when he visited the Court of England he took with him a handsomely-bound copy of his work; and, doubtless, if one could follow the good Canon one would find his journeys littered with similar copies which were probably expensive gifts to the recipient, for what return would a knightly soul make for a book which enshrined his own valor?

But without looking too curiously into his motives, it must be admitted that the work could not have been done more thoroughly. There is something of Herodotus in the Canon's cheery, chatty, garrulous, take-it-or-leave-it manner. But he has the advantage of the old Greek in accuracy. Considering that he belonged to the same age which gravely accepted the travelers' tales of Sir John Maundeville, it is, I think, remarkable how careful and accurate the chronicler is. Take, for ex-

ample, his description of Scotland and the
Scotch. Some would give the credit to Jean-
le-Bel, but that is another matter. Scotch
descriptions are a subject over which a four-
teenth-century Hainaulter might fairly be allowed a little scope for his imagination. Yet
we can see that the account must on the whole
have been very correct. The Galloway nags,
the girdle-cakes, the bagpipes—every little detail rings true. Jean-le-Bel was actually present in a Border campaign, and from him
Froissart got his material; but he has never at-
tempted to embroider it, and its accuracy,
where we can to some extent test it, must pre-
dispose us to accept his accounts where they
are beyond our confirmation.

But the most interesting portion of old
Froissart's work is that which deals with the
knights and the knight-errants of his time,
their deeds, their habits, their methods of talking. It is true that he lived himself just a
little after the true heyday of chivalry; but he
was quite early enough to have met many of

the men who had been looked upon as the flower of knighthood of the time. His book was read too, and commented on by these very men (as many of them as could read), and so we may take it that it was no fancy portrait, but a correct picture of these soldiers which is to be found in it. The accounts are always consistent. If you collate the remarks and speeches of the knights (as I have had occasion to do) you will find a remarkable uniformity running through them. We may believe then that this really does represent the kind of men who fought at Crecy and at Poictiers, in the age when both the French and the Scottish kings were prisoners in London, and England reached a pitch of military glory which has perhaps never been equaled in her history.

In one respect these knights differ from anything which we have had presented to us in our historical romances. To turn to the supreme romancer, you will find that Scott's mediæval knights were usually muscular athletes in the prime of life: Bois-Guilbert, Front-de-Bœuf, Richard, Ivanhoe, Count Robert—they all were such. But occasionally the most famous of Froissart's knights were old, crippled and blinded. Chandos, the best lance of his day, must have been over seventy when he lost his life through being charged upon the side on which he had already lost an eye. He was well on to that age when he rode out from the English army and slew the Spanish champion, big Marten Ferrara, upon the morning of Navaretta. Youth and strength were very useful, no doubt, especially where heavy armor had to be carried, but once on the horse's back the gallant steed supplied the muscles. In an English hunting-field many a doddering old man, when he is once firmly seated in his familiar saddle, can give points to the youngsters at the game. So it was among the knights, and those who had outlived all else could still carry to the wars their wiliness, their experience with arms, and, above all, their cool and undaunted courage.

Beneath his varnish of chivalry, it cannot be gainsaid that the knight was often a bloody-minded and ferocious barbarian. There was little quarter in his wars, save when a ransom might be claimed. But with all his savagery, he was a light-hearted creature, like a formidable boy playing a dreadful game. He was true also to his own curious code, and, so far as his own class went, his feelings were genial and sympathetic, even in warfare. There was no personal feeling or bitterness as there might be now in a war between Frenchmen and Germans. On the contrary, the opponents were very soft-spoken and polite to each other. "Is there any small vow of which I may relieve you?" "Would you desire to attempt some small deed of arms upon me?" And in the midst of a fight they would stop for a breather, and converse amicably the while, with many compliments upon each other's prowess. When Seaton the Scotsman had exchanged as many blows as he wished with a company of French knights, he said,

"Thank you, gentlemen, thank you!" and galloped away.   An English knight made a vow, "for his own advancement and the exaltation of his lady," that he would ride into the hostile city of Paris, and touch with his lance the inner barrier.   The whole story is most characteristic of the times.   As he galloped up, the French knights around the barrier, seeing that he was under vow, made no attack upon him, and called out to him that he had carried himself well.   As he returned, however, there stood an unmannerly butcher with a pole-axe upon the sidewalk, who struck him as he passed, and killed him.   Here ends the chronicler; but I have not the least doubt that the butcher had a very evil time at the hands of the French knights, who would not stand by and see one of their own order, even if he were an enemy, meet so plebeian an end.

De Comines, as a chronicler, is less quaint and more conventional than Froissart, but the writer of romance can dig plenty of stones out of that quarry for the use of his own little building. Of course Quentin Durward has come bodily out of the pages of De Comines. The whole history of Louis XI. and his relations with Charles the Bold, the strange life at Plessis-le-Tours, the plebeian courtiers, the barber and the hangman, the astrologers, the alternations of savage cruelty and of slavish superstition—it is all set forth here. One would imagine that such a monarch was unique, that such a mixture of strange qualities and monstrous crimes could never be matched, and yet like causes will always produce like results. Read Walewski's "Life of Ivan the Terrible," and you will find that more than a century later Russia produced a monarch even more diabolical, but working exactly on the same lines as Louis, even down to small details. The same cruelty, the same superstition, the same astrologers, the same low-born associates, the same residence outside the influence of the great cities—a parallel could hardly be more complete. If you have not supped too full of horrors when you have finished Ivan, then pass

on to the same author's account of Peter the
Great. What a land! What a succession of
monarchs! Blood and snow and iron! Both
Ivan and Peter killed their own sons. And
there is a hideous mockery of religion running
through it all which gives it a grotesque horror of its own. We have had our Henry the
Eighth, but our very worst would have been a
wise and benevolent rule in Russia.

Talking of romance and of chivalry, that
tattered book down yonder has as much between its disreputable covers as most that I
know. It is Washington Irving's "Conquest
of Grenada." I do not know where he got his
material for this book—from Spanish chronicles, I presume—but the wars between the
Moors and the Christian knights must have
been among the most chivalrous of exploits. I
could not name a book which gets the beauty
and the glamour of it better than this one, the
lance-heads gleaming in the dark defiles, the
red bale fires glowing on the crags, the stern
devotion of the mail-clad Christians, the *débon-*

naire and courtly courage of the dashing Moslem. Had Washington Irving written nothing else, that book alone should have forced the door of every library. I love all his books, for no man wrote fresher English with a purer style; but of them all it is still "The Conquest of Grenada" to which I turn most often.

To hark back for a moment to history as seen in romances, here are two exotics side by side, which have a flavor that is new. They are a brace of foreign novelists, each of whom, so far as I know, has only two books. This green-and-gold volume contains both the works of the Pomeranian Meinhold in an excellent translation by Lady Wilde. The first is "Sidonia the Sorceress," the second "The Amber Witch." I don't know where one may turn for a stranger view of the Middle Ages, the quaint details of simple life, with sudden intervals of grotesque savagery. The most weird and barbarous things are made human and comprehensible. There is one incident which haunts one after one has read it, where

the executioner chaffers with the villagers as
to what price they will give him for putting
some young witch to the torture, running them
up from a barrel of apples to a barrel and a
half, on the grounds that he is now old and
rheumatic, and that the stooping and straining
is bad for his back. It should be done on a
sloping hill, he explains, so that the "dear little
children" may see it easily. Both "Sidonia"
and "The Amber Witch" give such a picture
of old Germany as I have never seen elsewhere.

But Meinhold belongs to a bygone generation. This other author in whom I find a new
note, and one of great power, is Merejkowski,
who is, if I mistake not, young and with his
career still before him. "The Forerunner"
and "The Death of the Gods" are the only two
books of his which I have been able to obtain,
but the pictures of Renaissance Italy in the
one, and of declining Rome in the other, are in
my opinion among the masterpieces of fiction.
I confess that as I read them I was pleased

to find how open my mind was to new impressions, for one of the greatest mental dangers which comes upon a man as he grows older is that he should become so attached to old favorites that he has no room for the new-comer, and persuades himself that the days of great things are at an end because his own poor brain is getting ossified. You have but to open any critical paper to see how common is the disease, but a knowledge of literary history assures us that it has always been the same, and that if the young writer is discouraged by adverse comparisons it has been the common lot from the beginning. He has but one resource, which is to pay no heed to criticism, but to try to satisfy his own highest standard and leave the rest to time and the public. Here is a little bit of doggerel, pinned, as you see, beside my bookcase, which may in a ruffled hour bring peace and guidance to some younger brother—

" Critics kind — never mind!
Critics flatter — no matter!
Critics blame — all the same!
Critics curse — none the worse!
Do your best — —— the rest!"

XI

I HAVE been talking in the past tense of heroes
and of knight-errants, but surely their day is
not yet passed. When the earth has all been
explored, when the last savage has been tamed,
when the final cannon has been scrapped, and
the world has settled down into unbroken virtue and unutterable dullness, men will cast
their thoughts back to our age, and will idealize
our romance and our courage, even as we do
that of our distant forbears. "It is wonderful
what these people did with their rude imple-
ments and their limited appliances!" That is
what they will say when they read of our ex-
plorations, our voyages, and our wars.

Now, take that first book on my travel
shelf. It is Knight's "Cruise of the *Falcon*."
Nature was guilty of the pun which put this
soul into a body so named. Read this simple

record and tell me if there is anything in Hakluyt more wonderful. Two landsmen— solicitors, if I remember right—go down to Southampton Quay. They pick up a long-shore youth, and they embark in a tiny boat in which they put to sea. Where do they turn up? At Buenos Ayres. Thence they penetrate to Paraguay, return to the West Indies, sell their little boat there, and go home. What could the Elizabethan mariners have done more? There are no Spanish galleons now to vary the monotony of such a voyage, but had there been I am very certain our adventurers would have had their share of the doubloons. But surely it was the nobler when done out of the pure lust of adventure and in answer to the call of the sea, with no golden bait to draw them on. The old spirit still lives, disguise it as you will with top hats, frock coats, and all prosaic settings. Perhaps even they also will seem romantic when centuries have blurred them.

Another book which shows the romance and

the heroism which still linger upon earth is that large copy of the "Voyage of the *Discovery* in the Antarctic" by Captain Scott. Written in plain sailor fashion with no attempt at over-statement or color, it none the less (or perhaps all the more) leaves a deep impression upon the mind. As one reads it, and reflects on what one reads, one seems to get a clear view of just those qualities which make the best kind of Briton. Every nation produces brave men. Every nation has men of energy. But there is a certain type which mixes its bravery and its energy with a gentle modesty and a boyish good-humor, and it is just this type which is the highest. Here the whole expedition seem to have been imbued with the spirit of their commander. No flinching, no grumbling, every discomfort taken as a jest, no thought of self, each working only for the success of the enterprise. When you have read of such pri-vations so endured and so chronicled, it makes one ashamed to show emotion over the small annoyances of daily life. Read of Scott's blinded, scurvy-struck party staggering on to their goal, and then complain, if you can, of the heat of a northern sun, or the dust of a country road.

That is one of the weaknesses of modern life. We complain too much. We are not ashamed of complaining. · Time was when it was otherwise—when it was thought effeminate to complain. The Gentleman should always be the Stoic, with his soul too great to be affected by the small troubles of life. "You look cold, sir," said an English sympathizer to a French *emigré*. The fallen noble drew himself up in his threadbare coat. "Sir," said he, "a gentleman is never cold." One's consideration for others as well as one's own self-respect should check the grumble. This self-suppression, and also the concealment of pain are two of the old *noblesse oblige* characteristics which are now little more than a tradition. Public opinion should be firmer on the matter. The man who must hop because his shin is hacked, or wring his hand because his knuckles are bruised should be made to feel that he is an object not of pity, but of contempt.

The tradition of Arctic exploration is a noble one among Americans as well as ourselves. The next book is a case in point. It is Greely's "Arctic Service," and it is a worthy shelf-companion to Scott's "Account of the Voyage of the *Discovery*." There are incidents in this book which one can never forget. The episode of those twenty-odd men lying upon that horrible bluff, and dying one a day from cold and hunger and scurvy, is one which dwarfs all our puny tragedies of romance. And the gallant starving leader giving lectures on abstract science in an attempt to take the thoughts of the dying men away from their sufferings—what a picture! It is bad to suffer from cold and bad to suffer from hunger, and bad to live in the dark; but that men could do all these things for six months on end, and that some should live to tell the tale, is, indeed, a marvel. What a world of feeling lies in the exclamation of the poor dying lieutenant:

"Well, this *is* wretched," he groaned, as he turned his face to the wall.

The Anglo-Celtic race has always run to individualism, and yet there is none which is capable of conceiving and carrying out a finer ideal of discipline. There is nothing in Roman or Grecian annals, not even the lava-baked sentry at Pompeii, which gives a more sternly fine object-lesson in duty than the young recruits of the British army who went down in their ranks on the *Birkenhead*. And this expedition of Greely's gave rise to another example which seems to me hardly less remarkable. You may remember, if you have read the book, that even when there were only about eight unfortunates still left, hardly able to move for weakness and hunger, the seven took the odd man out upon the ice, and shot him dead for breach of discipline. The whole grim proceeding was carried out with as much method and signing of papers, as if they were all within sight of the Capitol at Washington. His offense had consisted, so far as I can re-

member, of stealing and eating the thong
which bound two portions of the sledge together, something about as appetizing as a
bootlace. It is only fair to the commander to
say, however, that it was one of a series of
petty thefts, and that the thong of a sledge
might mean life or death to the whole party.

Personally I must confess that anything
bearing upon the Arctic Seas is always of the
deepest interest to me. He who has once been
within the borders of that mysterious region,
which can be both the most lovely and the
most repellent upon earth, must always retain
something of its glamour. Standing on the
confines of known geography I have shot
the southward flying ducks, and have taken
from their gizzards pebbles which they have
swallowed in some land whose shores no human foot has trod. The memory of that in-
expressible air, of the great ice-girt lakes of
deep blue water, of the cloudless sky shading
away into a light green and then into a cold
yellow at the horizon, of the noisy companion-

able birds, of the huge, greasy-backed water animals, of the slug-like seals, startlingly black against the dazzling whiteness of the ice —all of it will come back to a man in his dreams, and will seem little more than some fantastic dream itself, so removed is it from the main stream of his life. And then to play a fish a hundred tons in weight, and worth two thousand pounds—but what in the world has all this to do with my bookcase?

Yet it has its place in my main line of thought, for it leads me straight to the very next upon the shelf, Bullen's "Cruise of the *Cachelot*," a book which is full of the glamour and the mystery of the sea, marred only by the brutality of those who go down to it in ships. This is the sperm-whale fishing, an open-sea affair, and very different from that Greenland ice groping in which I served a seven-months' apprenticeship. Both, I fear, are things of the past—certainly the northern fishing is so, for why should men risk their lives to get oil when one has but to sink a pipe in the ground.   It is the more fortunate then that it should have been handled by one of the most virile writers who has described a sailor's life.   Bullen's English at its best rises to a great height.   If I wished to show how high I would take that next book down, "Sea Idylls."

How is this, for example, if you have an ear for the music of prose?   It is a simple paragraph out of the magnificent description of a long calm in the tropics.

"A change, unusual as unwholesome, came over the bright blue of the sea.   No longer did it reflect, as in a limpid mirror the splendor of the sun, the sweet silvery glow of the moon, or the coruscating clusters of countless stars.   Like the ashen-gray hue that bedims the countenance of the dying, a filmy greasy skin appeared to overspread the recent loveliness of the ocean surface.   The sea was sick, stagnant, and foul, from its turbid waters arose a miasmatic vapor like a breath of decay, which clung clammily to the palate and dulled all the senses. Drawn by some strange force, from the unfathomable depths below, eerie shapes sought the surface, blinking glassily at the unfamiliar glare they had exchanged for their native gloom—uncouth creatures bedight with tasselled fringes like weed-growths waving around them, fathom-long, medusæ with colored spots like eyes clustering all over their transparent substance, wriggling worm-like forms of such elusive matter that the smallest exposure to the sun melted them, and they were not. Lower down, vast pale shadows creep sluggishly along, happily undistinguishable as yet, but adding a half-familiar flavor to the strange, faint smell that hung about us."

Take the whole of that essay which describes a calm in the Tropics, or take the other one: "Sunrise as seen from the Crow's-nest," and you must admit that there have been few finer pieces of descriptive English in our time. If I had to choose a sea library of only a dozen volumes I should certainly given Bullen two places. The others? Well, it is so much a matter of individual taste. "Tom Cringle's Log" should have one for certain. I hope boys respond now as they once did to the sharks and the pirates, the planters, and all the rollicking high spirits of that splendid book. Then there is Dana's "Two Years before the Mast." I should find room also for Stevenson's "Wrecker" and "Ebb Tide." Clark Russell deserves a whole shelf for himself, but anyhow you could not miss out "The Wreck of the *Grosvenor*." Marryat, of course, must be represented, and I should pick "Midshipman Easy" and "Peter Simple" as his samples. Then throw in one of Melville's Otaheite books—now far too completely forgotten—"Typee" or "Omoo," and as a quite modern flavor Kipling's "Captains Courageous" and Jack London's "Sea Wolf," with Conrad's "Nigger of the Narcissus." Then you will have enough to turn your study into a cabin and bring the wash and surge to your ears, if written words can do it. Oh, how one longs for it sometimes when life grows too artificial, and the old Viking blood begins to stir! Surely it must linger in all of us, for no man who dwells in an island but had an ancestor in longship or in coracle. Still more must the salt drop tingle in the blood of an American when you reflect that in all that broad continent there is not one whose forefather did not cross 3,000 miles of ocean. And yet there are in the Central States millions and millions of their descendants who have never seen the sea.

I have said that "Omoo" and "Typee," the books in which the sailor Melville describes his life among the Otaheitans, have sunk too rapidly into obscurity. What a charming and interesting task there is for some critic of catholic tastes and sympathetic judgment to undertake rescue work among the lost books which would repay salvage! A small volume setting forth their names and their claims to attention would be interesting in itself, and more interesting in the material to which it would serve as an introduction. I am sure there are many good books, possibly there are some great ones, which have been swept away for a time in the rush. What chance, for example, has any book by an unknown author which is published at a moment of great national excitement, when some public crisis arrests the popular mind? Hundreds have been still-born in this fashion, and are there none which should have lived among them? Now, there is a book, a modern one, and written by a youth under thirty. It is Snaith's "Broke of Covenden," and it scarce attained a second edition. I do not say that it is a Classic—I should not like to be positive that it is not—but I am perfectly sure that the man who wrote it has the possibility of a Classic within him. Here is another novel, "Eight Days" by Forrest. You can't buy it. You are lucky even if you can find it in a library. Yet nothing ever written will bring the Indian Mutiny home to you as this book will do. Here's another which I will warrant you never heard of. It is Powell's "Animal Episodes." No, it is not a collection of dog-and-cat anecdotes, but it is a series of very singularly told stories which deal with the animal side of the human, and which you will feel have an entirely new flavor if you have a discriminating palate. The book came out ten years ago, and is utterly unknown. If I can point to three in one small shelf, how many lost lights must be flitting in the outer darkness!

Let me hark back for a moment to the subject with which I began, the romance of travel and the frequent heroism of modern life. I have two books of Scientific Exploration here which exhibit both these qualities as strongly as any I know. I could not choose two better books to put into a young man's hands if you wished to train him first in a gentle and noble firmness of mind, and secondly in a great love for and interest in all that pertains to Nature. The one is Darwin's "Journal of the Voyage of the *Beagle.*" Any discerning eye must have detected long before the "Origin of Species" appeared, simply on the strength of this book of travel, that a brain of the first order, united with many rare qualities of character, had arisen. Never was there a more comprehensive mind. Nothing was too small and nothing too great for its alert observation. One page is occupied in the analysis of some peculiarity in the web of a minute spider, while the next deals with the evidence for the subsidence of a continent, and the extinction of a myriad animals. And his sweep of knowledge was so great, botany, geology, zoology, each lending its corroborative aid to the other. How a youth of Darwin's age—he was only twenty-three when in the year 1831 he started round the world on the surveying ship *Beagle*—could have acquired such a mass of information fills one with the same wonder, and is perhaps of the same nature, as the boy musician who exhibits by instinct the touch of the master. Another quality which one would be less disposed to look for in the savant is a fine contempt for danger, which is veiled in such modesty that one reads between the lines in order to detect it. When he was in the Argentine, the country outside the Settlements was covered with roving bands of horse Indians, who gave no quarter to any whites. Yet Darwin rode the four hundred miles between Bahia and Buenos Ayres, when even the hardy Gauchos refused to accompany him. Personal danger and a hideous death were small things to him compared to a new beetle or an undescribed fly.

The second book to which I alluded is Wallace's "Malay Archipelago." There is a strange similarity in the minds of the two men, the same courage, both moral and physical, the same gentle persistence, the same catholic knowledge and wide sweep of mind, the same passion for the observation of Nature. Wallace by a flash of intuition understood and described in a letter to Darwin the cause of the Origin of Species at the very time when the latter was publishing a book founded upon twenty years' labor to prove the same thesis. What must have been his feelings when he read that letter! And yet he had nothing to fear, for his book found no more enthusiastic admirer than the man who had in a sense anticipated it. Here also one sees that Science has its heroes no less than Religion. One of Wallace's missions in Papua was to examine the nature and species of the Birds-of-Paradise; but in the course of the years of his wanderings through those islands he made a complete investigation of the whole fauna. A foot-note somewhere explains that the Papuans who lived in the Bird-of-Paradise country were confirmed cannibals. Fancy living for years with or near such neighbors! Let a young fellow read these two books, and he cannot fail to have both his mind and his spirit strengthened by the reading.

XII

HERE we are at the final séance. For the last time, my patient comrade, I ask you to make yourself comfortable upon the old green settee, to look up at the oaken shelves, and to bear with me as best you may while I preach about their contents. The last time! And yet, as I look along the lines of the volumes, I have not mentioned one out of ten of those to which I owe a debt of gratitude, nor one in a hundred of the thoughts which course through my brain as I look at them. As well perhaps, for the man who has said all that he has to say has invariably said too much.

Let me be didactic for a moment! I assume this solemn—oh, call it not pedantic! —attitude because my eye catches the small but select corner which constitues my library of Science. I wanted to say that if I were advising a young man who was beginning life, I should counsel him to devote one evening a week to scientific reading. Had he the perseverance to adhere to his resolution, and if he began it at twenty, he would certainly find himself with an unusually well-furnished mind at thirty, which would stand him in right good stead in whatever line of life he might walk. When I advise him to read science, I do not mean that he should choke himself with the dust of the pedants, and lose himself in the subdivisions of the Lepidoptera, or the classifications of the dicotyledonous plants. These dreary details are the prickly bushes in that enchanted garden, and you are foolish indeed if you begin your walks by butting your head into one. Keep very clear of them until you have explored the open beds and wandered down every easy path. For this reason avoid the text-books, which repel, and cultivate that popular science which attracts. You cannot hope to be a specialist upon all these varied subjects. Better far to have a

broad idea of general results, and to understand their relations to each other. A very
little reading will give a man such a knowledge of geology, for example, as will make
every quarry and railway cutting an object of
interest. A very little zoology will enable you
to satisfy your curiosity as to what is the
proper name and style of this buff-ermine
moth which at the present instant is buzzing
round the lamp. A very little botany will enable you to recognize every flower you are
likely to meet in your walks abroad, and to
give you a tiny thrill of interest when you
chance upon one which is beyond your ken.
A very little archæology will tell you all about
yonder British tumulus, or help you to fill in
the outline of the broken Roman camp upon
the downs. A very little astronomy will
cause you to look more intently at the heavens,
to pick out your brothers the planets, who
move in your own circles, from the stranger
stars, and to appreciate the order, beauty, and
majesty of that material universe which is

most surely the outward sign of the spiritual force behind it. How a man of science can be a materialist is as amazing to me as how a sectarian can limit the possibilities of the Creator. Show me a picture without an artist, show me a bust without a sculptor, show me music without a musician, and then you may begin to talk to me of a universe without a Universe-maker, call Him by what name you will.

Here is Flammarion's "L'Atmosphère"—a very gorgeous though weather-stained copy in faded scarlet and gold. The book has a small history, and I value it. A young Frenchman, dying of fever on the west coast of Africa, gave it to me as a professional fee. The sight of it takes me back to a little ship's bunk, and a sallow face with large, sad eyes looking out at me. Poor boy, I fear that he never saw his beloved Marseilles again!

Talking of popular science, I know no better books for exciting a man's first interest, and giving a broad general view of the sub-

ject, than these of Samuel Laing. Who
would have imagined that the wise savant and
gentle dreamer of these volumes was also the
energetic secretary of a railway company?
Many men of the highest scientific eminence
have begun in prosaic lines of life. Herbert
Spencer was a railway engineer. Wallace
was a land surveyor. But that a man with
so pronounced a scientific brain as Laing
should continue all his life to devote his time
to dull routine work, remaining in harness
until extreme old age, with his soul still open
to every fresh idea, and his brain acquiring
new concretions of knowledge, is indeed a
remarkable fact. Read those books, and you
will be a fuller man.

It is an excellent device to talk about
what you have recently read. Rather hard
upon your audience, you may say; but without wishing to be personal, I dare bet it is
more interesting than your usual small talk.
It must, of course, be done with some tact
and discretion. It is the mention of Laing's

works which awoke the train of thought which led to these remarks. I had met some one at a *table d'hôte* or elsewhere who made some remark about the prehistoric remains in the valley of the Somme. I knew all about those, and showed him that I did. I then threw out some allusion to the rock temples of Yucatan, which he instantly picked up and enlarged upon. He spoke of ancient Peruvian civilization, and I kept well abreast of him. I cited the Titicaca image, and he knew all about that. He spoke of Quarternary man, and I was with him all the time. Each was more and more amazed at the fulness and the accuracy of the information of the other, until like a flash the explanation crossed my mind. "You are reading Samuel Laing's 'Human Origins'!" I cried. So he was, and so by a coincidence was I. We were pouring water over each other, but it was all new-drawn from the spring.

There is a big two-volumed book at the end of my science shelf which would, even now,

have its right to be called scientific disputed
by some of the pedants. It is Myers' "Human Personality." My own opinion, for
what it is worth, is that it will be recognized
a century hence as a great root book, one from
which a whole new branch of science will have
sprung. Where between four covers will
you find greater evidence of patience, of
industry, of thought, of discrimination, of that
sweep of mind which can gather up a thousand
separate facts and bind them all in the meshes
of a single consistent system? Darwin has
not been a more ardent collector in zoology
than Myers in the dim regions of psychic research, and his whole hypothesis, so new that
a new nomenclature and terminology had to
be invented to express it, telepathy, the subliminal, and the rest of it, will always be a
monument of acute reasoning expressed in
fine prose, and founded upon ascertained fact.

The mere suspicion of scientific thought or
scientific methods has a great charm in any
branch of literature, however far it may be

removed from actual research. Poe's tales, for example, owe much to this effect, though in his case it was a pure illusion. Jules Verne also produces a charmingly credible effect for the most incredible things by an adept use of a considerable amount of real knowledge of nature. But most gracefully of all does it shine in the lighter form of essay, where playful thoughts draw their analogies and illustrations from actual fact, each showing up the other, and the combination presenting a peculiar piquancy to the reader.

Where could I get a better illustration of what I mean than in those three little volumes which make up Wendell Holmes' immortal series, "The Autocrat," "The Poet," and "The Professor at the Breakfast Table"? Here the subtle, dainty, delicate thought is continually reinforced by the allusion or the analogy which shows the wide, accurate knowledge behind it. What work it is, how wise, how witty, how large-hearted and tolerant! Could one choose one's philosopher in the Elysian fields, as once in Athens, I would surely join the smiling group who listened to the human, kindly words of the Sage of Boston. I suppose it is just that continual leaven of science, especially of medical science, which has from my early student days given those books so strong an attraction for me. Never **have** I so known and loved a man whom I had never seen. It was one of the ambitions of my lifetime to look upon his face, but by the irony of Fate I arrived in his native city just in time to lay a wreath upon his newly-turned grave. Read his books again, and see if you are not especially struck by the up-to-dateness of them. Like Tennyson's "In Memoriam" it seems to me to be work which sprang into full flower fifty years before its time. One can hardly open a page haphazard without lighting upon some passage which illustrates the breadth of view, the felicity of phrase, and the singular power of playful but most suggestive analogy. Here, for example, is a paragraph—no better

than a dozen others—which combines all the
rare qualities—

"Insanity is often the logic of an accurate
mind overtasked. Good mental machinery
ought to break its own wheels and levers, if
anything is thrust upon them suddenly which
tends to stop them or reverse their motion. A
weak mind does not accumulate force enough
to hurt itself; stupidity often saves a man
from going mad. We frequently see persons
in insane hospitals, sent there in consequence
of what are called religious mental disturb-
ances. I confess that I think better of them
than of many who hold the same notions, and
keep their wits and enjoy life very well, outside of the asylums. Any decent person
ought to go mad if he really holds such and
such opinions. . . . Anything that is
brutal, cruel, heathenish, that makes life hope-
less for the most of mankind, and perhaps for
entire races—anything that assumes the neces-

sity for the extermination of instincts which
were given to be regulated—no matter by what
name you call it—no matter whether a fakir,
or a monk, or a deacon believes it—if received, ought to produce insanity in every well-
regulated mind."

There's a fine bit of breezy polemics for the
dreary fifties—a fine bit of moral courage too
for the University professor who ventured to
say it.

I put him above Lamb as an essayist, because there is a flavor of actual knowledge and
of practical acquaintance with the problems
and affairs of life, which is lacking in the elfin
Londoner. I do not say that the latter is not
the rarer quality. There are my "Essays of
Elia," and they are well-thumbed as you see,
so it is not because I love Lamb less that I
love this other more. Both are exquisite, but
Wendell Holmes is for ever touching some
note which awakens an answering vibration
within my own mind.

The essay must always be a somewhat repellent form of literature, unless it be handled with the lightest and deftest touch. It is too reminiscent of the school themes of our boyhood—to put a heading and then to show what you can get under it. Even Stevenson, for whom I have the most profound admiration, finds it difficult to carry the reader through a series of such papers, adorned with his original thought and quaint turn of phrase. Yet his "Men and Books" and "Virginibus Puerisque" are high examples of what may be done in spite of the inherent unavoidable difficulty of the task.

But his style! Ah, if Stevenson had only realized how beautiful and nervous was his own natural God-given style he would never have been at pains to acquire another! It is sad to read the much-lauded anecdote of his imitating this author and that, picking up and dropping, in search of the best. The best is always the most natural. When Stevenson becomes a conscious stylist, applauded by so many critics, he seems to me like a man who, having most natural curls, will still conceal them under a wig. The moment he is precious he loses his grip. But when he will abide by his own sterling Lowland Saxon, with the direct word and the short, cutting sentence, I know not where in recent years we may find his mate. In this strong, plain setting the occasional happy word shines like a cut jewel. A really good stylist is like Beau Brummell's description of a well-dressed man—so dressed that no one would ever observe him. The moment you begin to remark a man's style the odds are that there is something the matter with it. It is a clouding of the crystal—a diversion of the reader's mind from the matter to the manner, from the author's subject to the author himself.

No, I have not the Edinburgh edition. If you think of a presentation—but I should be the last to suggest it. Perhaps on the whole I would prefer to have him in scattered books, rather than in a complete set. The half is more than the whole of most authors, and not the least of him. I am sure that his friends who reverenced his memory had good warrant and express instructions to publish this complete edition—very possibly it was arranged before his lamented end. Yet, speaking generally, I would say that an author was best served by being very carefully pruned before being exposed to the winds of time. Let every weak twig, every immature shoot be shorn away, and nothing but strong, sturdy, well-seasoned branches left. So shall the whole tree stand strong for years to come. How false an impression of the true Stevenson would our critical grandchild acquire if he chanced to pick down any one of half a dozen of these volumes! As we watched his hand stray down the rank how we would pray that it might alight upon the ones we love, on the "New Arabian Nights," "The Ebb Tide," "The Wrecker," "Kidnapped," or "Treasure Island." These can surely never lose their charm.

What noble books of their class are those last, "Kidnapped" and "Treasure Island"! both, as you see, shining forth upon my lower shelf. "Treasure Island" is the better story, while I could imagine that "Kidnapped" might have the more permanent value as being an excellent and graphic sketch of the state of the Highlands after the last Jacobite insurrection. Each contains one novel and admirable character, Alan Breck in the one, and Long John in the other. Surely John Silver, with his face the size of a ham, and his little gleaming eyes like crumbs of glass in the center of it, is the king of all seafaring desperadoes. Observe how the strong effect is produced in his case, seldom by direct assertion on the part of the story-teller, but usually by comparison, innuendo, or indirect reference. The objectionable Billy Bones is haunted by the dread of "a seafaring man with one leg." Captain Flint, we are told, was a brave man; "he was afraid of none, not he, only Silver—Silver was that genteel." Or, again, where John

himself says, "there was some that was feared
of Pew, and some that was feared of Flint;
but Flint his own self was feared of me.
Feared he was, and proud.   They was the
roughest crew afloat was Flint's.   The devil
himself would have been feared to go to sea
with them.   Well, now, I will tell you.   I'm
not a boasting man, and you seen yourself how
easy I keep company; but when I was quar-
termaster, lambs wasn't the word for Flint's
old buccaneers."   So by a touch here, and a
hint there, there grows upon us the individuality of the smooth-tongued, ruthless, masterful,
one-legged devil.   He is to us not a creation
of fiction, but an organic living reality with
whom we have come in contact; such is the
effect of the fine suggestive strokes with which
he is drawn.   And the buccaneers themselves,
how simple, and yet how effective are the little
touches which indicate their ways of thinking
and of acting.   "I want to go in that cabin,
I do; I want their pickles and wine and that."
"Now, if you had sailed along o' Bill you

wouldn't have stood there to be spoke twice —not you. That was never Bill's way, not the way of sich as sailed with him." Scott's buccaneers in "The Pirate" are admirable, but they lack something human which we find here. It will be long before John Silver loses his place in sea fiction, "and you may lay to that."

Stevenson was deeply influenced by Meredith, and even in these books the influence of the master is apparent. There is the apt use of an occasional archaic or unusual word, the short, strong descriptions, the striking metaphors, the somewhat staccato fashion of speech. Yet, in spite of this flavor, they have quite individuality enough to constitute a school of their own. Their faults, or rather perhaps their limitations, lie never in the execution, but entirely in the original conception. They picture only one side of life, and that a strange and exceptional one. There is no female interest. We feel that it is an apothesis of the boy-story—the penny number of our youth *in excelsis*. But it is all so good, so fresh, so picturesque, that, however limited its scope, it still retains a definite and well-assured place in literature. There is no reason why "Treasure Island" should not be to the rising generation of the twenty-first century what "Robinson Crusoe" has been to that of the nineteenth. The balance of probability is all in that direction.

The modern masculine novel, dealing almost exclusively with the rougher, more stirring side of life, with the objective rather than the subjective, marks the reaction against the abuse of love in fiction. This one phase of life in its orthodox aspect, and ending in the conventional marriage, has been so hackneyed and worn to a shadow, that it is not to be wondered at that there is a tendency sometimes to swing to the other extreme, and to give it less than its fair share in the affairs of men. In British fiction nine books out of ten have held up love and marriage as the be-all and end-all of life. Yet we know, in actual practice, that this may not be so. In the career of the average man his marriage is an incident, and a momentous incident; but it is only one of several. He is swayed by many strong emotions; his business, his ambitions, his friendships, his struggles with the recurrent dangers and difficulties which tax a man's wisdom and his courage. Love will often play a subordinate part in his life. How many go through the world without ever loving at all? It jars upon us then to have it continually held up as the predominating, all-important fact in life; and there is a not unnatural tendency among a certain school, of which Stevenson is certainly the leader, to avoid altogether a source of interest which has been so misused and overdone. If all love-making were like that between Richard Feverel and Lucy Desborough, then indeed we could not have too much of it; but to be made attractive once more the passion must be handled by some great master who has courage to break down conventionalities and to go straight to actual life for his inspiration.

The use of the novel and piquant forms of

speech is one of the most obvious of Stevenson's devices. No man handles his adjectives with greater judgment and nicer discrimination. There is hardly a page of his work where we do not come across words and expressions which strike us with a pleasant sense of novelty, and yet express the meaning with admirable conciseness. "His eyes came coasting round to me." It is dangerous to begin quoting, as the examples are interminable, and each suggests another. Now and then he misses his mark, but it is very seldom. As an example, an "eye-shot" does not commend itself as a substitute for "a glance," and "to tee-hee" for "to giggle" grates somewhat upon the ear, though the authority of Chaucer might be cited for the expressions.

Next in order is his extraordinary faculty for the use of pithy similes, which arrest the attention and stimulate the imagination. "His voice sounded hoarse and awkward, like a rusty lock." "I saw her sway, like something stricken by the wind." "His laugh rang false, like a cracked bell." "His voice shook like a taut rope." "My mind flying like a weaver's shuttle." "His blows resounded on the grave as thick as sobs." "The private guilty considerations I would continually observe to peep forth in the man's talk like rabbits from a hill." Nothing could be more effective than these direct and homely comparisons.

After all, however, the main characteristic of Stevenson is his curious instinct for saying in the briefest space just those few words which stamp the impression upon the reader's mind. He will make you see a thing more clearly than you would probably have done had your eyes actually rested upon it. Here are a few of these word-pictures, taken haphazard from among hundreds of equal merit—

"Not far off Macconochie was standing with his tongue out of his mouth, and his hand upon his chin, like a dull fellow thinking hard.

"Stewart ran after us for more than a mile

and I could not help laughing as I looked back at last and saw him on a hill, holding his hand to his side, and nearly burst with running.

"Ballantrae turned to me with a face all wrinkled up, and his teeth all showing in his mouth. . . . He said no word, but his whole appearance was a kind of dreadful question.

"Look at him, if you doubt; look at him, grinning and gulping, a detected thief.

"He looked me all over with a warlike eye, and I could see the challenge on his lips."

What could be more vivid than the effect produced by such sentences as these?

There is much more that might be said as to Stevenson's peculiar and original methods in fiction. As a minor point, it might be remarked that he is the inventor of what may be called the mutilated villain. It is true that Mr. Wilkie Collins has described one gentleman who had not only been deprived of all his limbs, but was further afflicted by the insupportable name of Miserrimus Dexter. Stevenson, however, has used the effect so often, and with such telling results, that he may be said to have made it his own. To say nothing of Hyde, who was the very impersonation of deformity, there is the horrid blind Pew, Black Dog with two fingers missing, Long John with his one leg, and the sinister catechist who is blind but shoots by ear, and smites about him with his staff. In "The Black Arrow," too, there is another dreadful creature who comes tapping along with a stick. Often as he has used the device, he handles it so artistically that it never fails to produce its effect.

Is Stevenson a classic? Well, it is a large word that. You mean by a classic a piece of work which passes into the permanent literature of the country. As a rule you only know your classics when they are in their graves. Who guessed it of Poe, and who of Borrow? The Roman Catholics only canonize their saints a century after their death. So with our classics. The choice lies with our grand.

children.   But I can hardly think that healthy
boys will ever let Stevenson's books of adventure die, nor do I think that such a short tale
as "The Pavilion on the Links" nor so magnificent a parable as "Dr. Jekyll and Mr. Hyde"
will ever cease to be esteemed.   How well I
remember the eagerness, the delight with which
I read those early tales in "Cornhill" away back
in the late seventies and early eighties.   They
were unsigned, after the old unfair fashion,
but no man with any sense of prose could fail
to know that they were all by the same author.
Only years afterwards did I learn who that
author was.

I have Stevenson's collected poems over
yonder in the small cabinet.   Would that he
had given us more!   Most of them are the
merest playful sallies of a freakish mind.   But
one should, indeed, be a classic, for it is in
my judgment by all odds the best narrative
ballad of the last century—that is if I am
right in supposing that "The Ancient Mariner" appeared at the very end of the eight-

eenth. I would put Coleridge's *tour de force* of grim fancy first, but I know none other to compare in glamour and phrase and easy power with "Ticonderoga." Then there is his immortal epitaph. The two pieces alone give him a niche of his own in our poetical literature, just as his character gives him a niche of his own in our affections. No, I never met him. But among my most prized possessions are several letters which I received from Samoa. From that distant tower he kept a surprisingly close watch upon what was doing among the bookmen, and it was his hand which was among the first held out to the striver, for he had quick appreciation and keen sympathies which met another man's work half way, and wove into it a beauty from his own mind.

And now, my very patient friend, the time has come for us to part, and I hope my little sermons have not bored you over-much. If I have put you on the track of anything which you did not know before, then verify it and pass it on.   If I have not, there is no harm done, save that my breath and your time have been wasted.   There may be a score of mistakes in what I have said—is it not the privilege of the conversationalist to misquote? My judgments may differ very far from yours, and my likings may be your abhorrence; but the mere thinking and talking of books is in itself good, be the upshot what it may.   For the time the magic door is still shut.   You are still in the land of færie.   But, alas, though you shut that door, you cannot seal it.   Still come the ring of the bell, the call of the telephone, the summons back to the sordid world of work and men and daily strife.   Well, that's the real life after all—this only the imitation.   And yet, now that the portal is wide open and we stride out together, do we not face our fate with a braver heart for all the rest and quiet and comradeship that we found behind the Magic Door?

THE END

INDEX